BY DEBORAH ELLIS

FICTION

Looking for X
The Breadwinner
Parvana's Journey
Mud City
The Breadwinner Trilogy
A Company of Fools
The Heaven Shop
I Am a Taxi
Sacred Leaf
Jackal in the Garden: An Encounter with Bihzad
Jakeman
Bifocal (co-written with Eric Walters)
Lunch with Lenin and Other Stories

NONFICTION

Three Wishes: Israeli and Palestinian Children Speak
Our Stories, Our Songs: African Children Talk About AIDS
Off to War: Voices of Soldiers' Children
Children of War: Voices of Iraqi Refugees

NO SAFE PLACE

NO
SAFE
PLACE

DEBORAH ELLIS

GROUNDWOOD BOOKS
HOUSE OF ANANSI PRESS
TORONTO   BERKELEY

Groundwood Books / House of Anansi Press
110 Spadina Avenue, Suite 801, Toronto, Ontario M5V 2K4
or c/o Publishers Group West
1700 Fourth Street, Berkeley, CA 94710

We acknowledge for their financial support of our publishing program the Canada Council for the Arts, the Government of Canada through the Canada Book Fund (CBF) and the Ontario Arts Council.

Canada Council   Conseil des Arts   ONTARIO ARTS COUNCIL
for the Arts   du Canada   CONSEIL DES ARTS DE L'ONTARIO

Library and Archives Canada Cataloguing in Publication
Ellis, Deborah
No safe place / Deborah Ellis.
ISBN 978-0-88899-973-3 (bound).–ISBN 978-0-88899-974-0 (pbk.)
I. Title.
PS8559.L5494N57 2010   jC813'.54   C2010-901683-1

Cover photo: AFP/Getty Images
Design by Michael Solomon

Printed and bound in Canada

To those who can't get on the ferry.

ACKNOWLEDGMENTS

I'd like to thank Paul St. Clair of the Roma Community Center in Toronto, Maria Gailovà of Romodrom in Prague, the Iraqi refugee community in Amman, and my editor, Shelley Tanaka.

ONE

The sound of pissing woke him up.

Exhaustion had let Abdul slip into a half-sleep in spite of the pounding music from the disco up the street, but the tinkling of water hitting cement just a few feet away broke through his slumber.

He turned his head away.

He was well hidden in the shadows, down in the gully under the ruins of the old tower. The drunk couldn't see him, just disgust him.

The sound of a zipper, the uneven footfall staggering away. Abdul kept his eyes closed. If he didn't open them, maybe his brain would think he was still asleep and let him drift off again.

Then the disco music changed. A techno version of a Beatles song flooded the Place d'Armes. "Penny Lane."

Abdul didn't even try to get through it. He tossed back the filthy blanket, rolled it away into a corner and climbed the steps out of the gully, checking again to make sure the light chain with the thin medallion was still around his neck, under his clothes. He'd spend the rest of the night playing cat and mouse with the Calais police. It was a dangerous game, but it was a whole lot safer than remembering.

/ / / / / / / /

"How much?"

"Does it matter? It's more than you've got."

"You don't know how much I've got."

"I can smell you. Your stink tells the whole story."

Abdul clenched his toes inside his torn sneakers. It helped him control his temper.

At least my stink is honest, he thought, from months of hard travel and living rough. He wondered what the smuggler's excuse was.

"I'll owe you the rest," Abdul said.

The smuggler scratched himself in places that weren't supposed to be scratched in public. He exhaled cigarette smoke into Abdul's face.

"Don't like dirty Arabs."

"I'm Kurdish," Abdul said, then wanted to snatch the words back. He'd just played into the man's prejudice. Should he say that he was part Arab, his mother's family from Baghdad? Why bother.

"I'm sixteen," he said instead, lying just a little. "I'm

strong. I'll find work in England and pay you what I owe you." He spoke in English, which was better than his French. He knew the smuggler knew both.

"You'll work. You'll pay. You'll do as you're told."

My grandmother carried a gun in the mountains fighting for a Kurdish homeland, Abdul thought, and here I am in a back alley of Calais, negotiating with a fool.

"Just tell me how much," he said. "I'm too tired for games."

The smuggler spat on the ground, then held out his slab of a hand, wiggling his fingers.

Abdul dug down into his right front trouser pocket, the one with the pouch sewn inside it. He took out a roll of British pounds that had, until recently, been wrapped in plastic and shoved up his rectum. Not even that place was secure. He'd come across bodies with the bellies sliced open.

He took off the elastic band and put the bills in the smuggler's hand.

"Count it," Abdul said, "and give me a receipt."

The smuggler sneered and made Abdul's money disappear into his own pocket. He was a big man. He used to be muscled but had gone to flab, every meal he'd eaten attaching itself to his belly and his arms.

"You want a receipt, you little Kurd-turd? Ask the CRS. Get your receipt from them. And when you're finished, meet me tonight, two o'clock, where the campers park, back of the Au Côte d'Argent hotel. Do you know the place?"

Abdul knew it. It was by the pedestrian pier, where tourists stood to watch the ferries passing.

"Don't be late. I'd be happy to leave without you." The smuggler started to walk away. "You'll be eating lousy English food for breakfast."

Abdul was thin from too many months of being on the road, but strong from too many fights with other migrants. He flung himself at the smuggler's back, wrapping his arm so tightly around the bigger man's throat that the smuggler began to die, right there on his feet.

"Count it and give me a receipt," Abdul said.

The smuggler tried to shake him off, but his bloated body didn't function well without oxygen. He reached into his pocket and threw the wad of pound notes to the ground. Abdul released him and went after his money.

The smuggler's boot smashed into Abdul's head, sending him spinning into the gutter.

"Keep your money, Kurd-turd," he said as he stomped away. "I don't want you on my boat."

For a moment Abdul was too stunned to move. The kick, then his skull crashing into the curb put his brain on temporary lockdown. But he could feel his fingers, curled tightly around his money.

He let the smuggler go. There was no point running after him. Abdul had dealt with men like that in Iraq and all across Europe. They had no honor, and they could always find another customer.

His head was still buzzing, but he got to his feet anyway to escape the pile of dog dirt he'd nearly landed in. Everywhere in Calais, there was dog dirt. He used to wonder what was wrong with the French that they couldn't clean up after their dogs. Now he was beyond wondering. Now he just tried to watch where he stepped.

Abdul shoved the money back into his deep pocket without taking the time to rebind it. He'd have to find a place where he knew he was alone to roll it, wrap it in plastic and shove it back up his backside until he could find another smuggler. This alley looked deserted, but there could be people hidden among the garbage bins, waiting for their chance. He got out of there fast.

It had taken him weeks to find that smuggler. Calais was full of people eager to make money, but it was also full of cargo.

He could make another run at the Chunnel, the tunnel that went beneath the English Channel, and try to hop the razor-wire fence around the entrance, if he could find a place out of sight of the security guards and CCTV cameras. Maybe he could latch onto a freight train or even walk the fifty kilometers through the Chunnel.

Or he could try again to climb onto the back of a cargo truck headed for the ferry. For that, though, he needed courage, and his well of bravery had pretty near run dry. His previous attempts had ended with cuts and bruises, and he knew he had been lucky. The truck drivers were on to them now, and they would swerve wildly and deliberately to shake off any passengers.

He'd seen what had happened to other migrants. Broken bones, head injuries and deep cuts that went septic in the bad living conditions of the Jungle, the migrant camp.

The wad of money felt uncomfortable in Abdul's trousers. It was down deep, but it still felt within reach of thieves. Amassing it had cost him so much, and he'd never have the means to replace it. He had to keep it safe.

If he could at least close his pocket shut with safety pins, maybe he could leave his money there instead of shoving it into the other place.

But he had no safety pins. He kept his hand firmly in his pocket, on his money.

Abdul kept walking. It was dangerous to stand still. Someone could spot him and report him. But he walked without direction. Four months on the road, and he still hadn't conquered the problem of time. In Iraq there had never been enough time. Out on the road there was way too much, and no place to spend it.

The day had only just started, and the free meal wouldn't be served until early in the afternoon. Abdul decided to walk into town. Maybe there was someone looking for a day laborer — at half the legal wages, but it would still be money, money he could spend.

That was his rule. The money from Iraq was for getting into England. Anything else he needed on the way, he had to earn. That's why it had taken him four months to cross six countries.

Abdul changed directions. He'd been heading toward Sangatte, a suburb in the west of Calais with high sand dunes and long grass to hide in. He didn't stay long on the busy Avenue de Verdun, but turned down a side street and cut through the cemetery.

Calais was a pretty enough town. They worked hard at keeping it nice for the tourists coming and going from England. There was an old lighthouse and a war museum in an old Nazi bunker. The tower he'd slept under had been built in the 1200s, rattled by an earthquake in the 1500s, hit by a cannonball in the 1600s, bombed by the Germans in the 1900s, and pissed on by a drunk in 2009.

A breeze came off the Channel, and it caught him in such a way that it bounced off his clothes and drove his own scent into his nostrils. There wasn't much he could do about it. He had only what he was wearing and nowhere to do laundry.

The shops and hotels of Rue Royale came into view, but even as he approached them, Abdul knew he couldn't face asking for work. Calais had not been kind to him job-wise. He stuck out too much. All the migrants did. The people with money and passports were pink-cheeked and wore pastels. The migrants were the ones with the dark hair and dark skin and dark clothes.

He crossed the street and turned into Parc Richelieu. Sometimes he slept there on the soft grass, sheltered by low hedges. Not often, though. The police had taken to raiding the park in the middle of the night.

This morning it was quiet. Abdul sat on a bench and listened to the sound of the little waterfall. The sun found his bench and he started to doze.

Not for long. A group of drunken football fans stomped along the sidewalk, chanting loudly for their team. They didn't see him, but Abdul didn't want to wait for them to come back. It wasn't safe to stay in one place for too long.

He headed back toward town, but this time the Channel breeze brought with it the scent of croissants baking in the boulangerie. Abdul turned on his heels and walked away quickly. He was way too hungry to put up with that!

The sound of a police siren made him duck inside the nearest building. It was the public library. He hoped no one would kick him out. A library would be a good place to hole up for awhile.

A woman was sitting at the front desk. She kept her eyes on her work as Abdul came through the door.

He moved farther inside, into the rows of shelves. The library was quiet, with few people.

Why hadn't he come in before? History, travel, cookbooks, science, novels. Even children's books, with their bright pictures and promises of good tomorrows.

And then he saw words that were not in French. He thought he recognized Turkish. Then he saw Russian, and Farsi, and something he was pretty sure was Hungarian.

And then, on a single shelf, in a not-very-long row, he saw Kurdish.

Abdul took a book down from the shelf and read about mining, in his own language. He put that book back and read a fairytale, one he recognized from his grandmother. Then another book, about Kurdish history.

You are strong, his people seemed to be telling him. You will survive. You will carry us forward.

He hadn't realized he was grinning until he looked up and saw that the lady at the desk had a clear view of him, and she was smiling, too.

Abdul put the book back on the shelf and approached the desk.

"Please, do you have…?" He didn't know the French word for safety pins, but he saw one scattered among some stray paper clips. He picked it up, and was about to ask her if he could have it when she reached into a drawer and took out a whole container of them. She held it up so he could help himself. He took three, then took two more, and some elastic bands from the box on her desk.

He knew how to say thank you in French.

The librarian smiled again, then went back to her stack of books.

Abdul had spotted the sign for the men's room on his journey around the library. The first thing he did there was to roll his money back up in a tight bundle and wind the elastic bands around it. He fastened the pins over the opening to his deep pocket, locking the money inside. Then he washed himself quickly, even washing his hair, bending low over the sink and using pink hand soap from the dispenser.

He would have dried it under the hot-air hand dryer, but another patron came in at that moment, and Abdul didn't hang around.

He didn't mind that his clean, wet hair dripped water down his back. Outside the sun was shining, his money was secure, he felt almost clean, and he had read his own language.

Maybe he'd take another run at the Chunnel tonight.

But first, it was time to eat.

DEBORAH ELLIS

TWO

It was impossible to forget about the ferries. The hum of the motors and the foghorns announced their comings and goings. The terminal was a short walk from downtown, and with most of Calais slapped up against the Channel, the ferries were always visible.

Abdul felt like they were laughing at him.

He approached the grounds of the old warehouse where the meal would be served. Migrants were already gathering. A white man and woman passed him on the sidewalk, knocking his shoulder with their giant backpacks, dangling water bottles and paper sacks full of sandwiches from the boulangerie, laughing and looking at their street map. In a few hours they'd be in England, as easy as going for a walk — a walk to the ticket office, a walk onto the ferry, a walk into Dover.

Abdul couldn't even imagine what it would be like to be them.

The world is divided, he thought. Some people can get on the ferry. And some people can't.

The warehouse sat by the end of the train tracks, where Rue Margollé met the Boulevard des Alliés. A hundred or so migrants had set up camp there, hanging their washing and rained-on blankets over the barbs of the barrier fence to dry. They could almost spit on the ferries as they moved through the canal.

The parking lot by the loading dock was already filling up with migrants, even though it was early. This was when being small could be an advantage.

The food was always brought to the same location, to long folding tables set up in front of the loading dock of the warehouse. Abdul, checking the safety pins on his trouser pocket yet again to be sure they were still secure, started working his way in that direction.

The crowd was still in a gathering mood, and people let him move. Maybe today the charity would let him help serve. He'd been allowed to do it twice before. Even though it meant delaying his own meal – the scent of the hot rice and stew driving him crazy as he added a scoop of each to the thrust-forward plates – he would get an especially large portion at the end, and usually something extra. One time he'd been given a hygiene kit with a toothbrush and toothpaste and a little bar of fancy soap with the name of a hotel on it. Another time he'd been given a bar of chocolate, which he'd traded for bread.

The food was never late. Abdul appreciated that. Everything else in his life was uncertain. Maybe that was why the charity worked so hard to be dependable.

The charity van arrived. Abdul couldn't see behind him, but he could feel that the crowd had grown. It pushed forward as the big pots were lifted out of the back of the van. Always, there was the fear that there wouldn't be enough.

There were two big pots for each table. Abdul knew that one pot contained rice, and one pot contained stew. It was the same meal every day. Sometimes there was meat or chicken in the stew. Usually it was all vegetables.

He tried to squeeze his way to the front to ask for a serving job, but now the crowd was solid. They would not let him pass.

The lids came off the pots and the smell of the food was a signal for the crowd to push forward even more.

The charity people wore orange vests and tried to keep order.

"Take your plate, go out to your left," they said, trying to keep the human traffic flowing. But there were too many people. They were too hungry.

Abdul got his plate of food. He tried to reach for a plastic fork, but was shoved out of the way. Circling his plate with his arms, he moved to the left, trying to follow the rules. He saw a woman trying to shepherd her children at the next table. One child was shoved and his rice and stew spilled all over his clothes. The noise from the crowd was so loud that Abdul couldn't even hear the child's cries.

Abdul got away from the main crowd and started to eat, still standing, using his fingers to get the food to his mouth. He ate quickly. Having food stolen was not uncommon. He used the rice to encircle morsels of stew and didn't take his eyes off his plate until his tongue had lapped up everything.

This would be his last meal until tomorrow.

He looked up then at the crowd. It didn't seem to have gotten any smaller, even though he could tell from how deeply the ladles were going into the pots that the charity would soon run out of food. He began to look for an exit, but the only way off the quay was through the crowd.

He'd just reached the bin to toss away his plate when a roar rose up from the crowd. Abdul checked the tables. Food was still being served, but something was going on.

He scooted behind the servers and jumped up on the loading dock. From there he could look out over the crowd.

Something was happening in the middle of the lake of people. Bodies were bumping up against each other, the movements becoming harsher and rougher. In minutes the shouts turned to screams, and the edges of the crowd became wider as people in the middle tried to get away from the growing brawl.

"Who is it this time?" one of the charity workers asked Abdul as he jumped down to help her load the empty pots into the back of the van.

"I can't tell. Looks like everybody."

There were too many people in too small a space. The crowd by the tables was pushed from behind, shoving one of the charity workers right into the wall.

"That's it, clear away!" the woman in charge yelled. She had a voice like a megaphone.

It caused more panic. The people near the tables who had not yet been fed were desperate for food, and they saw their chance to eat being taken from them. One man took a pot that still had some rice in it out of the charity worker's hands. He tried to tell her that he would distribute it, that she should get into the van and be safe, but he didn't speak her language, and he had to yell to make himself heard through the crowd. All she heard was a man yelling at her and trying to take something out of her hands. She didn't understand. She screamed.

Abdul watched the tables collapse, the legs snap and the pots fall to the ground, spilling the food that was left. Hungry men, women and children tried to scoop up the food with their hands, swallowing stew with pebbles and dirt. Several people were stepped on. Their cries were lost under the trample.

Abdul stayed on the truck helping to load pots, giving a hand up to the distraught workers.

"It's the Afghans and Eritreans," one said. "An argument. Someone's been stabbed."

"We have to get in there," another worker said, digging out the first-aid kit.

"You can't. You can't get through."

"I'll help," Abdul said without thinking. If anything, he was smaller than the woman with the medical bag. "Stay behind me."

The woman grabbed firmly onto his jacket and they jumped down off the truck into the crowd.

Abdul plunged blindly, going against the wave of people, feeling backed up by the woman clutching his clothes.

"Medic!" he shouted in Arabic, in French and in Kurdish. "Clear the way — medic!"

Through the noise of the crowd came the noise of police sirens, the special sirens of the CRS, the security police. The sound that put terror into any migrant.

Abdul knew that whoever was wounded would be arrested before they were treated, and likely deported after that. He wanted to help get them out of there, so that when the CRS got to the middle of the crowd there would be no one they could take away. The police would beat at the crowd with batons, but migrants were tough. Many had been beaten before, often by people more brutal than the French.

By a miracle, the crowd parted enough to let Abdul and the woman through. The man on the ground was Eritrean. Blood came from a wound in his chest, and he was struggling to breathe.

The charity worker opened the first-aid kid and ripped open packets of gauze with her teeth.

"Hold this!" She pulled in volunteers to put pressure on the wound and carry the man to the truck.

Abdul could tell from the cries and the noise of pounding boots that the CRS was almost at them. He got ready to run.

Then he spied the knife – a serrated fish-gutter's knife – scuffling around under people's feet.

A knife like that would give him protection. He wouldn't even have to use it. He could just show it to people and they'd back away.

Scrambling on his hands and knees, he went after the knife. Several times he almost had it, then it would be kicked from his reach by the crowd on the move.

Finally his hand went firmly around the knife handle. Already he felt stronger. He held it tightly and got to his feet.

He brought the knife up just as a CRS officer moved in close to him. The knife stabbed into the officer's arm.

In that moment, Abdul saw the officer look at his face and memorize it through the protective plexiglass of his faceshield.

In the instant it took for the officer to raise his good arm, the one with the baton in it, Abdul ducked and plunged through the crowd.

He could hear the officers coming after him, could hear the cries of the migrants who closed ranks and were beaten for not getting out of the way. He heard, and he kept moving.

At the yacht basin, he jumped the low fence and stumbled his way down the stone steps, slimy from the seaweed left by the low tide. He tried to blend in with the wall as he made his way around the narrow ledge toward the steps in the opposite corner. The ledge was slippery, too, caked with seaweed and trash. But at least he couldn't be seen from above. And the few boats in the basin were abandoned by their owners this late in the season.

It was then that he noticed he was still clutching the knife. And it was covered with blood.

Abdul grabbed at an iron ring attached to the stone wall and leaned down, dipping the knife into the cold sea water. He wiped the blade and handle dry on his trousers and righted himself on the ledge.

The knife was too long to fit into his pocket and it was unsheathed, so it was dangerous to carry close to his body, and he certainly couldn't carry it out in the open.

For now he cupped the bottom of the handle in the palm of his hand and stuck the rest of it up his sleeve. He made his way over to the steps and headed up them.

He emerged from the basin by the old Fort Risban and kept walking toward the beach. Across from the boardwalk, an inflatable slide in the shape of the sinking ship *Titanic* looked depressed and out of air. The children who might have played on it were lined up at the ice cream trucks, whining in the chill breeze while their parents argued. The beach looked like a holiday, with beach huts and white sand, but Abdul knew how much dog dirt there was underneath that sand.

Away from the beach, in the high dune grass, Abdul found a child's T-shirt, discarded and dirty. He shook it free of dried seaweed and gravel.

"Mickey Mouse Christmas," he read, and he smiled at the cartoon with the big ears and the red hat. He took the knife, wrapped it in the T-shirt, then undid his shirt and stuck the bundle next to his skin. He would not be able to get at it quickly, but he felt better knowing he had it.

By the time the knife was hidden away and the last button on his shirt was refastened, Abdul knew one thing. He had stayed in Calais too long. He'd try to enter the Channel tunnel again that very night. And this time, he'd make it.

He needed a place to hide until it got dark. The officer he'd stabbed might be able to identify him. There was a chance he'd be recognized.

Lacking any better ideas, he headed toward the Jungle, doing his best to walk calmly, not to draw attention. He'd hide among the other migrants in the shantytown they'd erected in the forest out of packing crates and tarps. Even the police were afraid to go there.

Abdul could tell something was wrong when he was still half a mile away. Migrants were running and yelling, and he could smell smoke.

He started to run closer when he saw the riot police leading a convoy of bulldozers into the Jungle.

"They're flattening everything," a man called to him in Kurdish. "Don't go down there. You'll get your head broken."

Abdul joined his fellow Kurd, and they climbed a ladder attached to a warehouse wall. They went to the edge of the flat roof and sat, Abdul adjusting the knife next to his belly so he wouldn't stab himself.

"Mosul," the man said.

"Kirkut," Abdul told him, naming the place of his father's birth. It was easier that they were both Iraqi Kurds. They at least had a starting place to trust each other.

They said no more for a long while and just watched the destruction taking place below them.

Not that there was much to destroy. The shanties were constructed out of garbage, boards and plastic scrounged from the refuse tips or stolen from warehouse yards. Bits of plastic and cardboard were almost adequate in the summer, but it was now the middle of October. Surviving in them through the winter would be a gamble at best.

"At least it was somewhere," the Mosul man said, as if he was reading Abdul's thoughts. "It was a place where a man could say, 'I'm going home.'"

"Somewhere to go," Abdul agreed. He'd never had his own shack in the Jungle, but he'd made friends who let him sleep in theirs now and then. The shacks were scarcely more comfortable than sleeping on the street, and certainly no warmer. "Why now?"

"I heard that a woman was raped."

That didn't make sense. Women were raped all the time in the Jungle. The police didn't care.

"An English woman. Young. A journalism student," the man said. "Now they decide the Jungle is unsafe. Now they decide the Jungle is unhealthy. My little daughter died of pneumonia in our shack, but it wasn't unhealthy then."

"You have children?" Abdul asked, not even able to imagine what it would be like to live in the Jungle with children. He had only himself to take care of, and that was hard, every day.

"I had three. Now I have one. One of my sons was born with health problems, and he died. One of Saddam's bombs or one of Bush's bombs, who knows? Another bomb took my wife."

A gust of wind blew tear gas in their direction, searing Abdul's throat and making his eyes fill with water. He covered his face, closed his eyes, tried not to breathe and waited for the wind to change.

"What will you do?" he asked when the breeze shifted.

"There's talk of a hunger strike. Not just among the Kurds — among the Afghans, too, and the Iranians, and the Eritreans. A hunger strike in the middle of Calais, in Place d'Armes."

"What good would that do?"

"Some think it will shame the French and the rest of Europe into helping us."

"Europe would be happy if we all starved to death. Our dead bodies would be easy for them to deal with."

"I think shaming them is good. But a hunger strike wouldn't work. We don't have the solidarity. We're attacking each other instead of coming together."

As if to underline the point, the sound of an argument reached their ears from below. Two different groups, in two different languages, were fighting over some discarded cardboard they both needed to rebuild their shanties.

"What does the world expect of us?" the man asked. "When we are treated like animals, we become animals."

"Then what can we do?"

"My son and I are going to make our way to Paris, on foot if we have to — what's another long walk? We are going to the Eiffel Tower, or to that fancy garden with the flowers, or to the place where the president lives. I will get some gasoline, and I will pour it over my son and myself. Then I will tell him how much I love him. I will hold him close to me, and I will light a match."

Abdul wasn't shocked. But the man was making one big mistake.

"Spare your son," he said.

"For what? For this?" The man gestured at the chaos and misery below them.

"Take him to a mosque," Abdul said. "Or a synagogue

or a church. Leave him there with a letter from you that he can read when he gets lonely. Leave him with anything you still have that will remind him of you and where he came from. But leave him there, if you are determined to do this thing. The religious people will care for him. They'll find him a home."

"You think it's better he be cared for by strangers?"

"No, it's better he be cared for by you. Cared for, not set on fire."

"Go away. You are too young to know anything."

Abdul got to his feet. "Give your son a chance. If you don't like it here, go somewhere else."

"Good advice. Go follow it yourself. How long have you been here?"

Abdul stomped away. He was thinking hard.

After every raid or riot, there was a huge crush of people at the Chunnel entrance. The security police would be there in force tonight, too, and they'd be angry because one of their own had been stabbed. His chances of getting through were very small.

But he still had a way out.

The smuggler was leaving at two in the morning. Abdul knew the place the boat was leaving from.

All he needed to do was to keep hidden until then.

THREE

"If you give me a hard time, I will dump you in the Channel."

Abdul stood in the shadow between the canal wall and the light tower. Below him, almost close enough to touch, a small group of migrants were getting ready to make the final stage of their journey.

The smuggler repeated his warning in French, just to be sure he was understood.

"Now, give me your money."

Abdul counted heads. There was a family of five. They looked to be from Eritrea or Somalia. One of the children was a baby and would sit in its mother's lap. So the five of them would take up four spaces.

There was a teenaged girl, downplaying that she was a girl by tucking her long braid inside the back of her jacket. She wore a big hat pulled down around her face, and men's clothes that were loose and big around her. Clearly, though, she was a girl.

Five spaces.

There was a white boy, medium height, young looking but trying to look older by frowning. White men were unusual in the Calais migrant world, but not unheard of. There was a war in Georgia. There were wars in lots of places.

Six spaces.

A tall teenager, male, with Central Asian features, stood next to the white boy. Was he Tajik? Mongolian? Abdul couldn't tell. Maybe Afghan. He was hunched over and also frowning.

Seven spaces.

"Piglet! Get over here and help!"

A small boy, ten or eleven years old, came running up to the smuggler. His hair was long and unkempt.

The smuggler yelled at him in English.

"You're supposed to be working, not playing around. Is everything ready?"

"I…I think so." The boy spoke with a British accent.

"You think so. Useless brat. Get all this crap on the boat."

The boy struggled with the two bags the Eritrean family had with them.

The boy would take up a space. That made eight spaces. And the smuggler would take up a space. Nine spaces.

Abdul was going on that boat. He crept behind the dumpsters and looked down into the water.

The boat tied there was barely a bucket. It bobbed like a cork in the harsh waves smashing the old sea wall. Abdul counted out seating spaces for maybe six, if they all squished together. Even then, the boat would ride heavy.

Evidently, the Eritreans thought so, too. The husband and wife discussed it furiously, the money in the husband's hands, not yet relinquished to the smuggler. The smuggler got impatient and snatched the bills away.

"The boat is too small," the husband said. "The sea is too rough. My children..."

"You can always make more," the smuggler said. "You people breed like rats."

"We don't go," the husband said, his arm around his child. "We stay, find another boat. Return our money."

"Return your money? What do you think this is?"

"Our money," said the husband.

"What money? Did you give me money? Better call the police."

The tall young man with the Asian features stepped forward and took the smuggler by the arm.

The smuggler snorted and puffed.

"What do you think you're doing?"

The young man didn't answer, just took the money out of the smuggler's hand and gave it back to the Eritrean family. The smuggler glared hard at the young man, then signaled to the boy to get the family's bags off the boat.

"Enjoy the Calais winter, sleeping rough," he said to the family. "You'll wish you all died at sea."

To the tall young man he said, "You think you're going to paradise in England? You're going to hell — and I'll make sure it's a special one for you, you lousy Chinaman or whatever you are."

"Uzbek," said the young man, and he stepped back into the group.

"Uzbek," the smuggler spat. "That goes for all of you. None of you have enough money for the voyage. Jobs have been arranged for you in England and you belong to me until your debt is paid. If you give me a hard time, now or later, I will make you disappear, and don't think I can't do it. I'm not forcing you to come. Remember that. I didn't force you to do anything. You chose to be here, and you chose to agree to my terms."

Some choice, thought Abdul.

The smuggler raised his voice. "Hey, Piglet. Get over here!" The boy came running again. "This is my nephew. My lousy sister died and saddled me with him. He has a name, but it doesn't matter. To me he is a little pig eating my money." He bent down and made pig-snort noises in the boy's face. Then he knocked the boy to the ground with a wave of his big arm.

The migrants started to jump forward, but held themselves back.

"See how I treat my own flesh and blood? Imagine how

I will treat you out there on the open Channel, you who are not my family."

The boy got up from the dirt and hurried back to the wharf.

"Now, give me your money."

Abdul watched as the remaining migrants dug deep into pockets to bring out rolls of money – money that had made long journeys hidden in dark places, or had been earned with deeds too hideous to speak of. They had all come to the end of the land without arriving at a safe place. England was their last hope, but they could go no farther on their own.

The smuggler took the money from the Uzbek first. The boy looked about seventeen, and his shoulders drooped as if from exhaustion. Abdul saw him head down the steps to the boat, speak to the nephew and shake his hand.

Next was the white-skinned boy.

"You're fifteen?" the smuggler asked. "You look twelve. As long as you can work." The boy handed over his money. "No Communist tricks. Behave yourself, Boris."

"I am Russian, not Communist, and my name is Cheslav, not Boris."

"Who cares, Boris? Get in the boat."

Last to board was the girl. The smuggler stared at her with a hard and hungry look.

"The little Gypsy child," he said. "Welcome aboard,

sweetheart. If the journey gets dull, you can liven it up."

"I am fourteen, not a child. And my name is Rosalia, not sweetheart."

"Your voice I don't need. Keep it quiet and get in the boat."

Abdul watched the little boat fill up. He moved around the edges, from dark place to dark place, until he could see that the smuggler's attention was focused elsewhere. Then he stepped down into the boat and quickly scrunched himself onto a space beside Rosalia. The other migrants made room, and no one spoke.

The little boat was half a mile from shore, the thick fog already making the coast of France a thing of the past, when the smuggler realized there was one person extra.

"Who's that? Who are you?"

"I'm Abdul. You told me I could come."

"You're that dirty Arab, that Kurd. I told you that you could not come!"

"Well, here I am."

The smuggler started to stand, but that made the little boat rock even more in the choppy water. He could not keep his balance and sat back down again.

"Then we'll turn back. Boy! Turn us toward shore!"

The boy was back by the motor, his hand on the rudder. He looked around. "Which way is the shore?"

The fog was thick. The lights of France had vanished, and the lights of England were nowhere to be seen. The migrants clung to the benches they sat on, and waves tossed their little vessel.

"You are a fool, just like your mother was," the smuggler yelled at the little boy. "Just turn the boat around. Do I have to come back there?"

Instinctively, the migrants squished together to form a barrier in case he should try to pass through. One step and he could topple them all into the cold October water.

The boy at the back moved the rudder and the boat started to circle. The sea was against it. Waves smacked their faces and sent water flowing onto their clothes. The wind would not let them turn.

His uncle kept yelling, and the boy kept trying to make the turn.

"You will get us all killed," Cheslav yelled. "Try to get the rest of your money then, when you're at the bottom of the ocean!"

Water sloshed against their ankles, filling their shoes. The migrants tried to bail out by cupping sea water with their hands.

"Straighten that rudder," the smuggler ordered. "And pass up your money, Kurd, or jump off my boat."

"I'll pay you when we get to England," Abdul said. "If we get there."

The smuggler cursed and ranted, but the growing storm gave him little choice.

"I'll get your money," he said. "I'll get your money and

a whole lot else. You'll regret this. You can't cross me! I am a powerful man."

"You're a loud man, anyway," Abdul heard Rosalia mutter.

For awhile they seemed to be making progress, although it was dark and foggy and windy, and they could well have been going nowhere at all. The waves got bigger, sending the boat climbing to steep heights, then dropping it into deep troughs. The Uzbek was sick over the side.

The smuggler took a flask out of his jacket and poured its contents down his throat.

"You all think paradise awaits you in England," he said. "Think again. The British don't want you. The British don't want me and I was born there."

The more he drank, the more he switched his languages between English and French. He shouted sometimes and mumbled at others, so the migrants could not follow what he was saying. They could guess, though. They'd heard it all before.

"Sure, I bring you over the Channel for money," he said. "A man's got a right to earn a living. But I also do it for revenge. Each of you mongrels who lands on the Queen's soil is like a poke in the eye to Her Majesty." Then he sang some lines of "God Save the Queen," substituting "save" and "live" with words that were rude and vulgar.

On and on he went, ranting and drinking. He didn't even seem to notice when it started to rain.

Abdul pulled up the collar of his jacket, but the gesture meant nothing. He was already wet.

"And then on top of it, I get saddled with a kid. A useless insect of a kid. Afraid of his own shadow. Boy! Get up here!"

The boy didn't move. "I…the rudder…"

"Kurd-turd – you take the rudder. Send the brat up here."

"He can hear you from his seat," Abdul said. "We all can."

"Well, maybe I don't want you all to hear. Maybe I want a private moment between uncle and nephew."

"Then it would be better to do that on the shore," said Cheslav.

The smuggler reached out and slugged the Russian. His seatmate, the Uzbek, grabbed hold so he wouldn't go over the side.

"Hold it like this," the boy said to Abdul, handing him the rudder. "It's not hard."

"You don't have to go up there," Abdul said.

The boy didn't answer.

Balancing with his hands on the shoulders of the migrants, the boy walked the length of the little boat. The others kept him from falling as the boat rocked violently back and forth.

"Here he is," the smuggler said, grabbing the boy's arm. "The cause of all my sorrow. My Jonah, my millstone. I had a good life until you came along. I had a woman — you don't think I could get a woman, do you, mongrels? But the kid came along, and she left. 'You're work enough,' she said to me. 'I'm not looking after someone else's kid.'"

The smuggler's big hand went down on top of the boy's head. He tangled his fat fingers in the boy's long, fine hair. Even in the dark and the rain, Abdul could see the boy wince. But he did not make a sound.

"You're bad luck. You're an unwanted puppy, aren't you?" the smuggler said, bringing his face low and breathing his foulness right into the boy's nostrils. "You know what we do to unwanted puppies? We do to them what the sailors in the Bible did to their Jonah. We throw them overboard."

The next movements were swift and sudden and seemed to come from all over the boat.

The smuggler picked up the boy by his hair and moved to toss him out of the boat. At almost the same instant, the Uzbek jumped from his seat and flung himself at the smuggler.

The boat rocked viciously, the Channel water spilling in as each side dipped low.

"Bail!" yelled Abdul, but the others were already doing that, even while they screamed in fear.

The smuggler, clumsy and drunk, tried to shuck off his attacker.

A wave decided it. Over the bow went the three of them, the smuggler still clutching the boy. The big man fought the water, trying to keep himself afloat. He was forced to release his fingers from his nephew's hair. Every time he yelled and cursed, the sea flowed into his open mouth.

The boy was now loose, carried away by the sea. The Uzbek pushed off the smuggler, who had managed to grab hold, and went out after the boy, his long arms slamming through the waves.

Several times he just about grabbed the child, only to have the waves carry him away again. Finally, he took hold of the boy's jacket and held tight. They began the hard swim back to the boat, the Uzbek holding the boy's face out of the water.

There were oars in the boat. Cheslav and Rosalia held them out for the Uzbek to grab on to. Abdul steered the boat close to them, then cut the motor to hold it steady as the Uzbek pushed the boy out of the water for the others to haul back onto the boat. Then it was the Uzbek's turn, and the boat dipped perilously close to going right over as he reached up and climbed on board.

For a long moment, they could all do nothing more than breathe. Abdul took off his own jacket and put it around the boy, but everyone's clothes were more or less soaked, and the boat held no blankets.

Abdul had almost forgotten about the smuggler until he heard a voice roar up from the sea and felt a slap so hard on the side of the boat that the shudder ran up and down its spine. A fat hand appeared out of the depths and gripped the edge of the boat.

A second hand followed, and then it was as if Neptune himself was trying to climb into the boat. It tipped over almost ninety degrees and was edging to a complete flip when Cheslav took up an oar and smashed it down on the smuggler's hands. Abdul thought he could hear the bones break.

One hand released, and the boat began to right itself.

Rosalia picked up the other oar, and she and Cheslav whacked at the other hand until it was smashed and bloody. Abdul, his hands clutching Rosalia and Cheslav so he wouldn't fall over, kicked at the smuggler's head, smashing his nose, and pushed him away from the side of the boat. The oars pushed him farther away, and the waves did the rest.

It was barely a minute before the sea sucked away his screams and curses.

The migrants sat back down on the benches. No one spoke. The boy passed in and out of consciousness, and the Uzbek who had saved him shivered and shook in his wet clothes.

The rain came down and the waves carried the boat this way and that. Abdul could not get the motor re-started. The others tried, but they also had no luck. Without the motor, the rudder was useless.

The migrants huddled together so they could share what little warmth they had. They bailed out the boat with their cupped hands and scanned the sky for any signs of daylight.

Abdul was sure that every slap of a wave against the hull was the slap of the smuggler, caught up with them and ready for vengeance in the cold, dark night.

FOUR

Abdul was tired of huddling in the house.

Bit by bit, he headed toward the door, trying to be invisible. It wasn't easy. Not only did he have the handle of his guitar case tight in his hand, but there were wall-to-wall relatives packed into his parents' small house.

He'd been cooped up with them for more than two weeks while the earth shook and the sirens shrieked and Baghdad went up in flames. He'd tried his best to do the extra work his mother asked of him — the extra work brought on by all the people seeking refuge in their house because they thought it was in a safe neighborhood. He hadn't even complained — well, not too much — when his older cousins and brothers had gone out with the men to find supplies and he was kept at home by his mother, even though he was eleven and hardly a child.

But today was Wednesday. He'd already missed two Wednesdays with his guitar teacher, and he was not going to miss a third. All he needed to do was make it through the door.

It helped that the glass in the windows had been shattered by the explosions. The family had covered the windowpanes with flattened cardboard boxes and sheets of newspaper. It made the house darker than it would normally be. And since most of the bombs fell at night, people slept during the day. Abdul could see several sleeping relatives in each room he passed. He also had to be careful of his mother's paintings, taken down and stacked against the walls so they wouldn't be damaged when the house shook.

Holding his guitar carefully so it wouldn't knock into something and make noise, Abdul went step by step toward the door. He even held his breath.

From the back kitchen came the voices of his mother and her two sisters having a discussion about how many meals they could get out of the remaining flour and oil. With every second Abdul expected to be called on to fetch something or clean something.

But he made it to the door, then through it. He even managed to close the door behind him.

The small concrete yard was empty in the heat of the day, so Abdul had no problem crossing it and letting himself out through the high metal fence that separated their house from the street.

He stepped out into a city he didn't recognize.

It was as though God had picked up the world, shaken it madly, then let it fall through His fingers and scatter on the ground.

The men in his family should have prepared him. He should have been allowed to stay in the room when his brothers and older cousins came back with supplies and talked about the world outside. He should not have been sent out with the younger children.

The houses immediately around Abdul's house all had pieces missing. One had a huge hole in the roof. Another had a hole in the wall. Another had collapsed altogether. There were big chunks of cement and glass everywhere.

Abdul headed off in the direction of his teacher's street. He passed a home that had the whole front wall blasted away. Abdul could look into the open rooms. He saw an old man and woman sitting in the remains of their kitchen, looking at their hands.

He kept walking, the guitar bumping gently against his legs. The more he walked, the more rubble there was. He saw buildings that were still smoking and cars that were smashed and broken. He almost stepped on the body of a man that was badly burned, the mouth still open in its final scream.

Some neighborhoods were crowded with people scrambling through the wreckage, calling out to each other when they found food or a body. Others were trying to make crude repairs, shoring up their broken houses to get ready for the bombs to fall again.

When he got to his teacher's house, all that was left were hunks of concrete with steel rods sticking out of them like bones out of the remains of a fish. None of it was recognizable as walls or a roof.

Abdul could see the blue of the curtains — just a scrap — peeking out beneath the remains of a cookstove.

He called out his teacher's name.

"Bashar!"

There was no answer.

He called out the names of his teacher's family members – his wife, Maryam, his sons, Mohammed and Samir, and his little daughter, Fatima.

"Here I am," said a tiny voice. Abdul ran toward the sound.

"Fatima, is that you? Where are you?"

"I'm here," she said again. The sound came from above and to the back. He ran that way.

She was sitting on top of the rubble, clutching an orange and green pillow.

"It's your lesson day," she said when she saw it was Abdul. "Papa's not here."

"Where is he?"

She shrugged, then pointed down.

"Inside," she said. "I think they're inside. I didn't like the way the house shook. I brought my pillow to sleep outside.

Mama told me no, but I can do that sometimes." She tried to lift the slab of concrete that jutted into the one she was sitting on.

"It won't move," she said.

Abdul climbed up onto the rubble – difficult to do with one hand full of guitar. He sat down beside her.

"Has anyone come to help you?"

She just looked at him, her eyes big and round.

He tried to remember being five years old, but that was six whole years ago. A lifetime.

"Are you hungry?" he asked her. That was a safe question. Even five-year-olds knew if they were hungry or not.

She nodded.

"Come to my house. My mother will feed you."

"Will my mama and papa be there?"

He helped her climb down the rubble.

"It's my lesson day," he said. "If I don't show up, your father will know where to look for me."

He held her hand as they walked, and he wasn't at all embarrassed to be seen holding the hand of a little girl.

He had to walk her back through the rubble and destruction. To keep her busy and not scared, he taught her a song.

"This is by the Beatles," he said. "It's called 'Yellow Submarine.'"

Little Fatima did not know English, so he taught it to her in Arabic. The song still worked, and they sang it together all the way back to his house. Whenever he spotted a dead body, he made her sing especially loud so she wouldn't be afraid.

That night, Fatima sat in his mother's lap surrounded by all the relatives that Abdul now felt lucky to have around him — even his Uncle Faruk, who had majored in business and who his father said was allergic to joy. Fatima leaned back against his mother and laughed with the other little kids at the puppet show he and his father and cousins put together of Alice in Wonderland, with puppets made out of socks and cooking utensils. Abdul was playing the Queen of Hearts.

As he waited to make his entrance, he wrote his first song. It was about Fatima. He called it "The Girl on the Rubble," but in the song, the girl was not pointing down at the ruins. She was trying to touch the stars.

FIVE

It was a night without sleep. The rain fell without mercy, and the waves tossed the boat around like a plaything.

There were no lights to row toward and there was no rescue coming. No one on earth knew where they were, and no one had even noticed that they were missing.

The migrants clung to the boat, riding out the rise and fall of the waves.

Abdul tried to hold the rudder steady, but he didn't know why he bothered. He didn't think it was helping or hurting. The sea kept swirling.

"Bail out!" someone would yell, and everyone would bend and scoop, the waves easily replacing what they labored so hard to get rid of.

Dawn came slowly, hidden behind the thick clouds. By the time Abdul realized he could see, the rain had down-shifted from a deluge to a drizzle. The air was still cold and the wind still blew, but the waves rolled instead of rocked.

The migrants rolled with the waves and, exhausted from fear and shivering, they slept.

////////

"We killed the boy's uncle."

Cheslav's voice startled Abdul out of his slumber. It seemed to be around mid-morning. The rain was more mist than drops.

"It was self-defense," Rosalia said. "He would have tipped us over, climbing into the boat with his giant body."

"Who will care?" asked Cheslav. "We did it. The man was a pig, but he was all we had to guide us to England. Now we are stuck on the open sea in a piece of crap boat with a little boy who will turn us in as murderers. Boy, what kind of a boy are you?"

Abdul's arm was around the nephew's shoulder, trying to keep him warm. He could feel the heat from the boy's fever through his wet clothes.

"He's sick. Leave him alone."

"Soon. But we need to know. Is he the sort of boy who will cry to the authorities? Will he go, 'Boo-hoo, my uncle is dead and these are the people who killed him'? Or will he say it was an accident?"

"It was an accident," said Rosalia. "It was. Until we smashed his fingers."

"And those smashed fingers will still be attached to his

body when it washes up somewhere. There will be questions. What will the answers be?"

"Can't this wait?" Abdul asked.

"For what? We could be picked up at any time. His body could be fished out of the water at any time. Maybe there is something in his pockets to tie him to us. He has our money. Maybe he has something else."

"Like what?"

"I don't know! A list with our names on it? I did not come all this way to end up in a British jail. I can see that the boy is sick. It will not make him sicker to answer a question."

"We will all say he fell off the boat," Rosalia said. "We will keep our mouths shut about the broken fingers and the kicks to his head."

"It's the boy they will listen to. He's one of them." The Russian crouched down in front of the boy. "You are young, but you are old enough to look us in the eye and say what is in your mind. Do you want to put us in jail for killing your uncle?"

The nephew raised his head. His eyes met Cheslav's.

"I'm all alone."

"So are we. What's your answer?"

"You all saved my life," the boy said. "Especially him." He nodded at the Uzbek, who hadn't moved or spoken during the whole discussion. "I won't send you to jail."

Cheslav straightened up. "You hear that? That's a good,

strong answer. If we are caught and questioned, we will all say his uncle fell off the boat, and we know nothing about how he got injured. Are we all agreed?"

Abdul and Rosalia agreed.

"What about you, Uzbek?" Cheslav put a hand on his shoulder. "You're the big hero. What do you have to say?"

The Uzbek slumped under the pressure of Cheslav's hand. Abdul knelt beside him and looked in his face.

"I think he's dead."

"He's not dead! He can't be."

"I know what dead looks like. Come and see."

Cheslav and Rosalia looked. The tall young man had died.

"It was the cold," Abdul said, "and the wet. And maybe the fear."

"What should we do?" Rosalia asked.

"We throw him into the sea," said Cheslav. "We can't sail into England with a dead body in the boat."

"We didn't even know his name," said Abdul. "What are you doing?"

Cheslav was taking the jacket off the dead boy. "This is a warm jacket, warmer than mine. He doesn't need it anymore."

"That doesn't make it right."

"Look around you. None of this is right."

Cheslav maneuvered the Uzbek's arms out of the sleeves and spread the jacket out to dry.

Abdul sighed heavily. He bent down and undid the boots the dead boy was wearing. They were in much better shape than his own shoes.

"What's in the wallet?" Rosalia asked Cheslav, who was taking a small black wallet out of the inside pocket of the Uzbek's jacket.

"Don't worry. I'll share it with you."

"I mean, is there a name?"

Cheslav opened the wallet. In the place where the money would have been there was a photo of a man, a woman and three children, all dressed up and stiffly posed on a sofa. There was also a folded piece of paper.

"No money." He carefully unfolded the wet paper. "It's a letter."

"You can read Uzbek?" Abdul asked.

"Uzbekistan used to be part of the Soviet Union. They still speak Russian there." Cheslav read the note to himself.

"What does it say?" Rosalia asked.

"It's from his mother," Cheslav said. "What do you think it says?" He tossed it into the sea.

"Was there a name on it?"

"No."

"So we can't write to her," Abdul said. "She'll never know what happened to her son."

"If she wanted to know, she would have kept him with her," said Cheslav.

"We should have a service," Rosalia said. "We should say some prayers. We should say goodbye with respect."

"From Uzbekistan, he was probably a Muslim," said Abdul. "I am also Muslim. We should lay him out and pray before we send him on his way."

Rosalia used the Uzbek's neckerchief to cover his face. Abdul said a Muslim prayer. Rosalia said the Our Father in Polish and Cheslav prayed in Russian.

"Do you know any prayers?" Rosalia asked the boy.

"I'm sorry," he whimpered.

"Why are you sorry?" Abdul asked. "This is not your fault."

"I've been bad luck since I was born. My uncle was right. I'm a curse."

"Your uncle was a bad man," said Rosalia. "No one cares what he said."

"I'm bad luck."

Cheslav threw up his arms. "Little boy, we are all alone on the ocean with no working motor, no map, no food, no water, no papers, no dry clothes, and no home. Why do you think an unimportant child like you could make our lives any worse?"

"It's my name. My name is Jonah."

Everyone stared at him, and for awhile, no one spoke.

It was the Russian who started laughing.

The others watched him, stunned, and then, one by one, they joined in.

"What's so funny?" demanded the boy. "Don't laugh at me!"

"We're all going to die out here," said Cheslav. "After all we have been through, you really think your name is what gives us our bad luck?"

Jonah wiped his eyes and stopped crying. He almost smiled.

"Let's finish this," Abdul said. "Let's say goodbye to this Uzbek with no name. I think I would have liked him."

"I don't know any prayers," Jonah said. "But I know a Christmas carol."

He sang "Silent Night" while they lifted the Uzbek up and out of the boat. They placed him in the water as gently as they could. For a little while his body floated next to the boat, until the waves took it in one direction and the little boat went in another.

"Sleep in heavenly peace.

Sleep in heavenly peace."

SIX

"We should row," Rosalia said.

The sea was calm enough now that rowing might actually get them somewhere.

"Which way?"

The sky was a little lighter on one side of the horizon, under the clouds.

"That way is east," said Abdul. "England is west. We row toward England."

The boat had two oars. Abdul took the first shift, turning the boat with some difficulty. He had never rowed before, and he did a great deal of pulling without seeming to get anywhere.

"Oh, this is much better," Cheslav said. "We are really moving now."

"Shut up," said Rosalia.

"We will row and we will row and maybe in a month we will reach England. Maybe we are off-course and we'll row right by England, right into the middle of the Atlantic Ocean."

Abdul kept pulling on the oars. It felt like he was moving the boat along, but how could he say for sure? Maybe for every meter he moved them, the waves and currents moved them two, and in a direction they didn't want to go.

"How big is the Channel?" he asked Jonah. "How long does it usually take you to cross it?"

"We leave when it's dark and get there when it's light. If the motor is working."

"Where do you land?"

"Different places. Sometimes a bigger boat comes out to meet us and takes away the cargo."

"The cargo? You mean us?"

"No. The bundles under the floorboards."

Abdul, Cheslav and Rosalia looked at each other.

"Are there any bundles on this trip?" Cheslav asked.

"Sure."

"Where?"

Jonah pointed to places around the hull. "Under the boards."

Cheslav tried to pry up the boards with his fingers.

"Hey. Gypsy, got a nail file?"

Rosalia ignored him.

Abdul secured the oars, reached into his shirt and unwrapped the knife.

"You're going to kill me for my words?"

Abdul didn't answer. He bent to one of the floorboards and started attacking it with the knife.

"You've never used a knife before, have you?" Cheslav taunted. "The boat is made of wood, not cake."

Abdul swung his arms up so the knife point was at Cheslav's throat.

"I stabbed a security officer. I'm not afraid to stab you."

"Go ahead and try," Cheslav urged. "You want to be king of the boat? Try. You don't know me."

Abdul lowered the knife and went back to attacking the board. It started to loosen. The boat tipped precariously as they all leaned in to look.

Jonah was the one who reached in and grabbed the two packets.

Wrapped in heavy, clear plastic, each was about the size of a deck of cards.

"Heroin?" Abdul asked. "Cocaine?"

"It's heroin," Jonah said. "I heard them saying."

"How many are there?"

Jonah showed them the spots. "Three hiding places."

Abdul didn't know how much money was involved, but he knew it was a lot. "We should throw it away."

"Are you crazy?" Cheslav asked. "Before this, we had nothing. Now we are rich. And, if we're caught, we have something to bargain with."

"If we're caught with drugs, we'll go to prison," said Abdul.

"I will not get caught," Cheslav said. "I will turn this into money. When I have money, it will be easy to do what I want to do."

"What's that?"

"None of your business."

Abdul was already tired of the Russian. He handed Cheslav his knife. "You want to work instead of talk?"

Cheslav took the knife and chopped at the places Jonah showed him. One by one, six heroin packets were uncovered.

"Any more?" Cheslav asked.

Jonah shook his head.

Abdul took the knife back.

"So we have heroin," he said. "So what? It's not food, it's not water. It won't fix the motor or keep us dry. It's useless."

"I'll take your share, then," Cheslav said.

"You can have it," Abdul said. "I want nothing to do with it."

Cheslav grabbed Abdul's share and tucked it along with his own into his waistband behind his back.

Rosalia picked up one packet and put it down again.

"I don't like trouble," she said.

Jonah reached for a packet but Abdul stopped him.

"Leave it in the boat. It's not going anywhere."

"Why should the boy get a share?" Cheslav asked. "His country will take care of him."

"It belongs to him as much as to you," Rosalia said, as she took up the oars and got them moving again.

The sun climbed higher and the clouds began to drift

away. The day warmed up. Abdul allowed his body to relax and his mind to drift.

Cheslav was fooling himself if he thought the heroin would save him. Abdul would throw Jonah's share overboard before he allowed the boy to leave the boat with it.

Stop worrying about him, he told himself. He reminded himself that he had something to do. He had to get to England, and then he had to get to Liverpool. And he couldn't let anything get in his way.

SEVEN

Abdul woke up, and for a moment he didn't know where he was.

He'd been dreaming he was a small boy, visiting his grandparents in the Kurdistan countryside. He was chasing a baby goat, running over the rocky hills and laughing in the sunshine.

But when he opened his eyes, the little farm was gone, the goat was gone, and the sun was gone. Everything was dark, and he was cold once again.

He'd slept slumped over, and his back and neck ached. He yawned and stretched, then rubbed his eyes.

He was looking at another boat. They had drifted right into it.

It was a cabin cruiser, a yacht, four times longer than their little boat and many times higher.

Even in the dark, Abdul could see it was expensive. Tiny lights twinkled here and there along its sides.

Abdul nudged Cheslav and Rosalia awake and

motioned to them to be quiet. Jonah stirred but didn't quite awaken. Abdul could tell from his fever and labored breathing that the boy was really sick.

"Should we shout out for help?" he wondered.

"Why would they help us?" whispered Rosalia.

"They're all asleep up there," said Cheslav. "We go up, we get blankets, water and food. We take what we need, and then we get back on our own boat and row away."

"I'll go," said Abdul. "One of us is enough."

"Why would I trust you? I'll go." Cheslav was already on his feet, securing their boat to the yacht.

"I'm going," said Rosalia. "I won't waste time, and why would I trust you?"

"Someone should stay with Jonah," Abdul said.

"You think he'll run away?" Cheslav was already pulling himself onto the yacht after Rosalia. Abdul followed him.

Empty liquor bottles littered the deck.

On one of the cushioned benches they saw a man, passed out and snoring.

"I'm going below. You go round the back," Cheslav whispered to Rosalia. He told Abdul to check out the wheelhouse.

Abdul didn't like to be ordered around by Cheslav, but this was no time to argue. He went to the little covered deck that held the ship's wheel and control panel.

There were more bottles and paper plates with the

remains of a meal. Abdul picked up a half-eaten chicken leg and finished it off in two bites. There was a roll, and some kind of cold potatoes in sauce. It felt great to eat, but then he felt bad when he remembered the goal was to get things they needed and get away.

He spied some large bottles of drinking water. There were four unopened bottles and one that was still half-full. On the back of one of the chairs was a sweater, and two towels were bunched up on the floor. He used the larger towel to bundle up what he found.

Abdul looked around carefully for anything else they might use. Whoever owned this boat had a lot of money. The console was full of fancy electrical equipment. He thought he recognized a radio and gears, but most of it was a mystery.

They needed to find out where they were, and how far away they were from England.

We could get there quickly in this, Abdul thought. The man who owned the yacht could take them to England easily, but Abdul knew he never would.

He figured he'd taken all that was useful, and he was just turning to go back to the others when he heard a shout from below.

He froze.

There was another shout, then another. At first they were just shouts of surprise. Then they were shouts of anger.

Up from below came Cheslav, and right behind him

was a man with white hair and a thick body, wearing an open bathrobe over his boxer shorts. The man held a pistol pointed at Cheslav's back.

"We have a thief," the man said, in English with an American accent. "Came right up onto our boat, Harry. Right into my bedroom! Trying to steal my wallet!"

"I was after your blanket," Cheslav said. "It was on the floor. You didn't even need it."

"Are you all right, Frank?"

"I caught me a baby pirate," said the man with the gun.

Harry grabbed Cheslav and spun him around so that he leaned against the yacht's railing, looking out at the black sea. The man kicked his legs apart and started to pat him down, searching him. It took no time at all to find the heroin packed away in Cheslav's clothes.

"You worked narcotics, Frank," said Harry, bending down to pick up the packets that fell out of Cheslav's shirt. "How much do you think this is worth?"

"On the streets of Detroit? It would sure pad out my pension."

"You still have your old contacts?"

"I could find them. Their lives don't change."

"That's mine!" yelled Cheslav, taking a swing at Harry.

Shut up, thought Abdul, as Harry punched Cheslav hard in the stomach. The Russian fell to his knees.

Abdul tried to get at his knife. He knew what was coming. These men had no reason to keep Cheslav alive. It would be only moments before they discovered the rest of them. He wondered where Rosalia was, and hoped she was well hidden.

Harry pulled the belt out of the loops of his bathrobe and wound them around Cheslav's wrists, pulled back tight from his shoulders.

"Where did you get this?" Frank demanded, speaking inches from Cheslav's face. "How did you get on my boat? Tell us, and maybe you'll live to get to a police station."

Cheslav took a deep breath and spat right in Frank's face. Frank cursed, and the two men hit and kicked the boy, Frank using his gun instead of his fist.

Abdul got ready to jump. Out of the corner of his eye he saw Rosalia holding an oar, poised to attack.

"There's more!"

Abdul heard Jonah's voice, then saw him on the yacht's deck.

The men stopped beating Cheslav and turned to Jonah.

"What is this — nursery school? Where did you come from?" Frank grabbed Jonah and threw him to the deck beside Cheslav.

"There is more heroin on our boat," said Jonah, his face flushed from fever and his hair matted with sweat and salt. "Lots more. Go and see for yourselves."

Frank stood up and kept his gun aimed at the boys.

"Go check it out," he said to Harry.

Harry, keeping a tight hold on the two packets of heroin

he'd found on Cheslav, walked to the other side of the yacht.

"There's a beat-up old motorboat down here. It's empty."

"The drugs are hidden," Jonah said. "I can show you."

"Hold it." Frank used his free hand to pat down Jonah and check him for weapons. "Show us," he told Jonah. "From up here, and no tricks!"

Jonah went to the side of the yacht and told Harry where to look.

"Frank! You've got to see this!"

"Don't move," Frank said to Cheslav. He joined Jonah at the side of the boat and leaned over to get a better look.

Abdul moved fast. He ripped the knife from his clothes, ran to the side and pushed Frank over the railing. He heard a thud and a splash as the large man landed half in the skiff and half in the sea. It took just a second to cut through the rope tying the two boats together.

At that same moment, he heard the sound of the yacht's motor starting.

Frank and Harry scrambled to get back onto their boat.

"Let's go!" yelled Cheslav.

"Haul up the anchor!" yelled Rosalia from the wheelhouse.

Abdul stayed at the side with his knife, ready to fight the men if they managed to climb up. The yacht slowly started to move, creating a three-foot gap, then a six-foot gap, then a ten-foot gap. The men might have made it if they'd acted immediately, instead of trying to pick up all the heroin first.

They could still swim, Abdul thought. They'd have to leave the drugs, but they could still make it.

"Help me!"

Jonah was struggling to haul up the anchor by hand. Abdul quickly sliced through Cheslav's bindings. Cheslav, his face bloodied from the beating, stumbled over to help Jonah with the anchor, and Abdul ran back to the side of the boat.

The extra person on the anchor was helping. The yacht was moving a little faster. Rosalia was having some trouble with the controls. Their getaway wasn't smooth, but every moment put more distance between them and the men.

"You damn kids!" Harry yelled. "You damn, worthless, good-for-nothing…kids!!" He spat out the last word as if it was the worst curse ever.

Frank fired his gun at them but his shots were wide. The yacht picked up speed.

Within moments, their fortunes had changed.

Abdul yelled back. "Yes, we are kids. We are unwanted, worthless, useless children. But," he laughed, "we have your boat!"

He felt the adrenalin rush through his body. He felt in control of his life for the first time in a long, long time. And he also felt something else, something he hadn't felt in years.

It may have been joy.

EIGHT

"Open the door!"

Abdul heard hard banging and the sound of the front door being smashed in.

His head thick with sleep, he tried to jump to his feet, but the soldiers were already upon him. They swarmed into the front room that was now his bedroom, ripped him off the mat and shone a flashlight in his face, blinding him.

"Don't move!"

"Show us where the weapons are!"

"Who are you hiding here?"

"You asked those same questions the last time you broke our door," Abdul said, in English because he knew the Americans didn't understand Arabic. He heard the cries of the small children and the screams of the women from deeper inside the house.

"It's all women back here!"

"Where are the men?"

A soldier pulled Abdul up into a sitting position and got right close to his face.

"Where are they?"

"You killed them all," Abdul said.

The soldier slapped him so hard he fell over.

"Bag him."

A hood was yanked down over Abdul's head and his hands were pulled behind him. A soldier kneeled into his back and wrapped plastic handcuffs around his wrists.

Abdul screamed in pain as he was lifted by his arms and dumped outside. He was made to sit with his head bowed against the front wall of the house. He tried to get to his feet but a heavy hand on his shoulder made it impossible for him to rise.

"If there's anything in there, we'll find it, Ali."

"My name is Abdul."

"Whatever. How old are you?"

"Thirteen."

"Tell me now where the weapons are and there will be a reward in it for you. What would you like?"

"We have no weapons."

"There's only women in there," another voice said.

"Some kind of brothel?"

"They're all widows," Abdul told them. "And their children. My mother took them in so they'd be safe."

"What about your father?"

"My father is dead. My older brothers are dead."

"So you're the man, then."

Abdul didn't respond. He felt like a small boy. He was in his pajamas, shivering in the cold Baghdad night, and he could do nothing to help his mother or himself.

He could hear the women, less afraid and more angry now that they were fully awake.

"Where's my son?" his mother yelled. "What have you done with Abdul?"

There was more yelling, then the voices of the women and children became muted. Abdul guessed that they had all been locked in the kitchen. That's what usually happened during these night raids. He had never been tied up like this, though. He tried to calm himself the way his father had taught his theater students who were nervous before a performance.

"Curl your toes and breathe deeply," his father had told them. "Be aware of your surroundings. Try to own the moment."

It was hard to breathe deeply with the hood covering his face. The cloth stank. How many others had tried to catch their breath inside it?

The Song of the Hood, he thought. He could write a song about a hood that goes from prisoner to prisoner. Maybe he'd give it a happy ending, and the hood could land on one of the soldiers who was now breaking whatever unbroken furniture was left in his house.

The exercise was working. Writing songs always

made him feel better. A melody started working its way into his head — a melody that began dark and sad but became triumphant at the end when the tormentor became the prisoner.

Then Abdul heard music coming from a guitar.

His guitar! The soldiers were going to steal his guitar!

"That's mine!" he yelled. "The guitar is mine. Get your hands off it!"

"What's an Arab kid want with a guitar? Don't they play camel bones or something?"

"This your guitar, kid? Untie his hands."

Abdul, his hands freed, was turned around so his back was against the wall. He felt the guitar land in his lap.

"Play us a song, kid. Brighten up our humdrum lives."

Abdul's left hand curved around the neck of the guitar and his right hand found the strings. He was trembling, too frightened to remember anything he knew. Then he got angry, and he started to play.

"All we are saying," he sang through his hood, "is give peace a chance."

Over and over. He didn't bother with the verses, just kept on with the chorus until the guitar was yanked out of his hands.

"Enough of that hippy stuff. Let's have some heavy metal!" The soldier, who couldn't play, plucked the strings so harshly Abdul was afraid they would break. He had no idea how he would get new ones.

"What's going on here? Stop that noise!"

Abdul heard the guitar being snatched from the rough soldier's hands.

"Any weapons found? Why is this boy wearing a hood?"

The hood was lifted off.

"He was slow to obey orders, Sergeant."

"So are you, Private. Go join the others."

The sergeant squatted down in front of Abdul and lightly strummed the strings, slipping into a bit of a melodic riff.

"You a Beatles fan?"

Abdul didn't answer.

"George Harrison was just about the best guitar player there ever was." The sergeant played the opening to "Here Comes the Sun." He smiled at Abdul. "It hurt me when he died." He thumped his chest where his heart was covered by his uniform, his bulletproof vest and his ammo belt.

Abdul just watched him.

The sergeant sighed and handed the guitar back. He helped Abdul to his feet.

"Your mother's inside, son. Try to get some sleep."

Abdul watched as the soldiers moved on to torment the people in the next house. Then he went inside to help his mother calm the children and put their house back together.

No one got any more sleep that night.

A few days later, Abdul was driving with his mother in

a borrowed car. Fatima sat between them in the front seat. She was now seven years old, and Abdul's mother couldn't go anywhere without her. She'd stopped talking after the rocket attack that killed Abdul's father and brothers, and she was so quiet that Abdul sometimes forgot she was there — until she got more than a few feet from his mother. Then she'd wail like a siren.

His mother now wore hijab, which she had never done before, because women with their hair uncovered were being threatened.

"With it or without it, I am still who I am," she told Abdul when he asked her about it. "With it, I can do my work. What else is there to think about?"

"You've got to watch your mouth," she said to him now as she slowed down at an army checkpoint. The soldiers peered into the car before waving them along. "You make smart remarks, you're going to get into trouble."

"I get into trouble anyway," Abdul said.

"Do you want me to have another thing to worry about?"

"I'm not a child."

"You are my child, and I am going to protect you until we are both old and gray."

"You're already old and gray," Abdul said. His mother laughed and gave him a little swat on the head.

"My son is a bad boy," she said to Fatima, who looked up at her with big eyes. "But we have to love him anyway."

She eased the car through traffic to the curb in front of a restaurant.

"Mr. Hassan has a bag of onions for us," she said.

Abdul got out of the car. The onions would be chopped up by the widows living in his house, added to other donated food and made into cheap meals for a few of Baghdad's hungry.

"We won't get rich," his mother often said, "but we're staying alive. In Iraq today, that is a victory."

Abdul got the onions and discreetly checked them to make sure they weren't rotten. He was effusive in his praise for Mr. Hassan's generosity.

"Everyone will give more when they feel appreciated," his mother often said.

It worked with Mr. Hassan. He added a bag of hard lemon candies.

"To make the children happy," he said.

Abdul thanked him again and left when he saw that no other treats were being offered. He put the onions into the back of the car and climbed into the front seat.

"I have a surprise for you," he said to Fatima. He handed her a candy. She smiled.

"Mr. Hassan said the candy would make the children happy," Abdul told his mother.

"If only that's all it took," his mother replied. She checked the road, then drove away from the curb.

They had not gone very far when they were stopped by

a car driving across the road in front of them. Abdul's mother leaned on the car horn but the car in front didn't move.

Another car pulled up close to Abdul's door, so close that his door could not open. The men inside were staring at him.

"Mama…"

His mother tried to turn the car to get them out of there, but she was stopped by a car that pulled up on her side.

She threw the car into reverse and stepped on the gas, smashing into the car that was now tight in behind them.

Two men in black ski masks came out of the car by his mother's side. They each held a machine gun. They pointed their guns at Abdul's mother.

"Only whores drive!" one of the men shouted.

Then they opened fire.

Abdul flung himself down on the seat, over top of Fatima. He clawed the air, trying to grab his mother to pull her down out of the range of the bullets.

There was shattered glass everywhere. The guns were loud and seemed to go on and on.

And then there was silence. The guns stopped shooting. Abdul heard car doors slam, tires squeal and cars drive away.

"Mama? Mama!"

His mother's face was a mass of blood and pulp.

Little Fatima, leaning against his mother, was silent and still. There was a bullet hole in her head.

Abdul began to scream. He screamed and screamed and tried to shake his mother back to life.

His car door opened and hands reached for him. He fought them off but they pulled him out anyway and dragged him onto the sidewalk.

Abdul was blind with fear and sorrow. He curled up into a ball and cried. He felt himself being lifted gently and held by a stranger whose arms wrapped around him and held him close.

He cried and cried.

When he finally stopped crying long enough to look at who was holding him, he realized it was a boy not much older than himself.

"I'm Kalil," the boy said. "Cry all you want. My mother is dead, too."

NINE

Abdul walked the deck.

The sun was up, and the water was calm. He recognized and appreciated the sweetness of the moment. He'd been here before — this brief juncture when immediate danger had passed, pressing needs were met, and the work of the next step had not yet begun. It was time to breathe, to feel the sun, to tend to wounds and not think too deeply.

Soon after their getaway, Jonah had collapsed. He'd just slipped to the floor as though his legs had turned to jelly. He was down below now, piled in bed with blankets. The yacht was well stocked with everything, including medicines. Abdul found some pills he recognized as being for fever. He crushed two of them, mixed them into a spoonful of strawberry jam from the kitchen and gave it to Jonah in small amounts. He made hot tea and held the boy's head while he drank it.

The men had also left lots of clothes. They were big men, and the clothes were big, but they were warm and dry and clean. The pockets of the trousers Abdul was wearing were deep. He'd transferred his money, pinned the pocket closed, and found a belt to hold them up. He had on a clean shirt, too, and a sweater that buttoned down the front and had a crest on the pocket.

The cabin cruiser had a small bathroom with a little shower in it. Rosalia had already used it, washing her long hair and emerging smelling of soap and shampoo. Abdul was waiting for more water to heat up before he took his shower. He'd had enough of cold water for awhile.

Cheslav was up at the wheel, wearing a sort of captain's hat he'd found in the cabin. He waved Abdul over.

"How is the boy?" he asked.

"He's sleeping. His fever is down, I think."

"He is still a problem."

"No more than the rest of us. Less, because he is British. When we land in England someone will take him in."

"Someone who will ask questions. 'Where is your uncle? Why are you alone? Who did you come here with?'"

"Jonah said he doesn't want us to go to jail. He's old enough to know how to keep his word."

"Nobody keeps their word."

"Well, then, maybe we'll get a reward," Abdul suggested, although he didn't really think they would.

"If they catch us, they will charge us with murder," Cheslav said. "They won't listen to us. Maybe they won't even listen to the boy. And now we have those Americans to worry about. We stole their boat."

"We'll just have to get to England and disappear before they are picked up," said Abdul.

"There's always one more thing to worry about."

Abdul knew what he meant. There always seemed to be one more thing. Solve one problem, and another one cropped up. Find transportation, then run out of food. Find food, then get stuck behind a border. Find a forger to get a passport made, then lose a friend in a train accident. One problem was fixed and a new one was created. Always one more thing.

Abdul left the Russian alone.

Rosalia was in the bow, spreading out wet clothes to dry in the sun.

"You did some laundry?" Abdul asked. Rosalia ignored him. "What about my clothes?" He'd dumped his dirty clothes on top of the pile that Cheslav had started on the floor of the small bathroom.

Rosalia looked up at him, glared, then went back to spreading out her own freshly washed clothes over the chairs. They would dry quickly in the sun and the breeze.

Abdul left her alone, too, and went below. Maybe there was enough hot water now for a shower. If not, he'd shower anyway. And wash his clothes.

Cheslav was the loudest, but it looked like Rosalia

might be the fiercest. He wasn't going to ask her again to do his laundry.

The water was a little warm. Abdul used lots of soap, then got back into his new clean clothes. His dirty clothes, the ones he'd traveled in from Iraq, were still on the floor. He scooped them up, then scooped up Cheslav's, too. If they were all going to survive, they would have to do things for each other.

Rosalia was in the little kitchen beside the bathroom.

"Use seawater for the washing. Just rinse them in fresh water," she ordered, and tilted her head toward the cupboard with the bucket and laundry soap. "I don't know how much fresh water we have."

"Thanks," said Abdul.

"The little boy's clothes are in the bedroom."

Abdul's arms couldn't hold anything more, so he dumped his and Cheslav's laundry up on deck and made a second trip. There was a rope attached to the handle of the bucket. He lowered it into the sea.

He washed his own clothes first. They hadn't been washed in such a long time, it took several buckets of water and lots of rubbing before they seemed clean.

He was used to looking after himself on the road, but it had been a long time since he'd looked after other people. Not since Iraq.

He'd missed it. It felt normal. This is what people did when they weren't on the run.

Clean clothes are so important, he thought, remembering how badly he'd smelled when he'd walked through the library. When we wear clean clothes, we feel like we belong. We feel like we have a right to —

"How much soap are you using?"

"What?"

Rosalia was standing over him, peering into the box of detergent.

"You use too much."

"I know how to wash clothes."

"I'm making a list," she said, "of everything we have. Finish here. We'll have tea and talk. Do Kurds drink tea?" She left without waiting for an answer.

"We drink more tea than Gypsies," Abdul muttered, then changed it to Roma even though no one could hear him. He knew from his time with migrants that many considered the word Gypsy to be insulting. He fiercely wrung out Jonah's shirt and shook it out before spreading it on deck.

Orders from Cheslav, orders from this girl — was this how it was going to be?

He was just finishing up when Rosalia came up on deck with a tray of tea and food.

"Get Cheslav," she said. "I suppose he has an opinion, too."

Cheslav was still at the wheel. The motor was off, but he sat at the controls. He was fiddling with the radio dials, trying to get a clear signal.

"Rosalia wants to talk," Abdul said. "We have things to decide."

"I make my decisions alone."

"Stay here, then. We'll make the decisions without you. She made sandwiches and we can certainly eat those without you, too."

Abdul walked away. In a moment, he could hear Cheslav following him.

They met on the bigger of the two decks. Cheslav looked at his freshly washed clothes.

"Who touched my things?"

"I washed them when I washed mine."

"I know how to wash clothes. Leave my things alone."

Cheslav took each piece of his wet laundry and straightened it out, smoothing out the wrinkles and folding creases into the trousers. Then he picked up a sandwich and started eating.

Abdul poured out the tea and thanked Rosalia for making it. She seemed surprised.

They'd all been eating steadily since coming on board the yacht, so they were no longer so ravenous that they jumped on the food, but there was always room for another meal. They'd all known too much hunger to pass up a sandwich.

"We have food for a week," Rosalia said, "if we do not stuff ourselves. And there are two fresh water tanks. One is full, one half full. We will use them only for drinking and cooking, and they will last."

"The fuel tank is at three quarters," Cheslav said. But no one knew how big the tank was or how much fuel it would take to get them to England.

"Where are we?" Abdul asked him. "You've been behind the wheel. You must know where we are."

"Why don't I use the radio and ask someone? I could call out in my Russian accent and ask for directions to Buckingham Palace."

"Can't you be pleasant?" Rosalia asked. "Why do you argue about everything?"

Cheslav made kissing noises at her.

In the next instant, Cheslav was flat on his back and Rosalia's foot was on his throat.

"I am tired of pig men," she said. She leaned her weight into his windpipe. Cheslav choked and gasped for breath and tried to push Rosalia off, but she held steady.

"Let him up," Abdul said, going to her side. "That's enough. He will leave you alone."

Still, Rosalia kept standing on the Russian's throat. Abdul saw something in her eyes. An anger — no, a rage — a rage so deep it had turned from fire to ice.

"There's been enough death," Abdul said to her. "We all need each other, for now."

Abdul watched Rosalia thinking. Then she moved her foot.

"For now," she said, and backed away.

Clutching his throat, Cheslav shrugged off Abdul's

attempts to help him to his feet. He stomped to the other end of the yacht.

"We need to find out where we are," Abdul said. "We need to know that we're headed in the right direction."

"So do it, then," was all Rosalia said, before she, too, stomped away.

Abdul went below to check on Jonah, the one person on the yacht who might be in a good mood. The boy was awake and out of bed, wandering around the little kitchen. The men's clothes, large on everyone, were comical on him, flapping around his arms and ankles.

"What are you doing up?"

"I had to use the toilet. All that tea."

"Back under the covers." Abdul helped him wrap up. "How is your throat?"

"Sore."

Abdul felt the skin on the boy's forehead. "Your fever is down."

"I'm sorry to be sick."

"Being sick is nothing to apologize for."

Abdul went into the kitchen. The refrigerator had a tiny freezer. There were ice cubes. He got some out, put them between the folds of a towel and smashed them against the counter. He put the ice chips in a bowl.

"Try these," he said, offering them to Jonah.

Jonah took a mouthful of the ice.

"Why are you doing this?"

"Doing what?" Abdul asked.

"Being nice to me."

"It's what people do."

The little cabin bedroom was a mess from everyone going through it to find things they needed. Abdul started to tidy it up.

The yacht was their home now. If he ever had another home, he would want to keep it tidy. He folded sweaters and socks away into drawers, and hung shirts on hangers in the little closet.

"I heard shouting," Jonah said.

"There was an argument."

"I don't like shouting."

There was a small wicker chair beside the bed. Abdul sat down.

"I don't know what to say about your uncle."

"I didn't like him."

"He was your family."

"I didn't like him."

Abdul nodded and absentmindedly smoothed out one of Jonah's blankets. "Do you have any other family?"

"My mother is dead. I never knew my father. My uncle said my mother was a whore."

"Your uncle was a liar."

"How do you know?"

"I met him. You must not think bad things about your mother. Is there anyone else? Any grandparents or uncles?"

"No. There was just us."

Abdul nodded, and they sat in silence for awhile.

"I'm hungry," said Jonah.

Rosalia had left a sandwich for Jonah in the kitchen. Abdul watched the boy grimace as the bites of sandwich went down his sore throat. Then Jonah went back to sleep.

It was that sort of day. There was work to be done and decisions to be made, but it seemed all that would have to wait. It was a day for eating and sleeping and not thinking too much.

Abdul went up on deck. He sat in the sun among the drying laundry and picked up a magazine. There was a man on the cover holding a large fish and looking very pleased with himself. Abdul practiced his English reading skills for awhile, then got up to wander the boat.

Everyone, it seemed, was sleeping — Jonah down below, Cheslav in the seat by the captain's wheel, his cap pulled down over his eyes, and Rosalia in one of the chairs by her laundry.

Someone should stand watch, Abdul decided, in case the coastguard or someone else was looking for them. But the chair across from Rosalia looked too inviting. He sat down on it.

A small plastic bag with tiny, shiny black stones was on the table beside her.

Abdul picked it up. He looked at Rosalia.

All the tension and rage were gone from her face. In her sleep, it looked like all was well.

TEN

"This is a smart girl."

Mr. Kruger made no sign that he had heard Uncle Nikolas's words. He kept tapping his feet and looking bored.

"This is a very smart girl," Uncle Nikolas repeated, "and I say that not because she is my niece, but because it is true. Only six years of schooling, but she has picked up many things on her own. Mathematics, she can do in her head. At just fourteen! Languages. Polish, English, Czech, and since we got your kind invitation, even a little German! You treat her right, she can earn good money for you." He put his arm around Rosalia's slim shoulders.

Mr. Kruger gave a jerk of his head toward the waiting car.

"It's a long drive," he said. "Let's go."

"Now, we have an agreement," Uncle Nikolas reminded him. "You will take my niece into Germany where she will work in your factory. You will find her a safe place to live and to go to school in the evenings, and for this service she will pay you a portion of her earnings. We have an agreement."

"Say your goodbyes," Mr. Kruger said. He picked up the small taped-up suitcase that held Rosalia's few things, headed over to the car and put it in the trunk.

Uncle Nikolas slowly steered Rosalia over to the car.

"Our family lived in Germany for hundreds of years before the war," he said to her. "You have never been there, but, in a way, you are going home."

"We carry our home in our hearts," Rosalia said, determined not to cry. "My mother taught me that." Before she died. Before Rosalia's father died and her older brothers scattered to the four winds in search of work.

Mr. Kruger honked the car horn. They were out of time.

Uncle Nikolas kissed Rosalia on the forehead and whispered an old Roma prayer in her ear. "Remember what you came from, and remember what you are worth," he said and pushed her away. She turned, but not before she saw his tears.

They did not waste time saying they would keep in touch.

"In the back," Mr. Kruger said, "and don't chatter."

Rosalia already had a pretty good idea what kind of man Mr. Kruger was. She'd seen where his eyes had gone when he looked at her. She was glad not to have to sit beside him, and she certainly didn't want to waste any of her precious thoughts or words on him.

She was not sad to be leaving the cluster of hovels on the edge of the Czech village. It was close to the great city of Prague, but it may as well have been on the far side of the moon. No running water, no heat, no real toilets. It was worse, even, than the place where she'd grown up, in Nowa Huta, the huge industrial suburb just outside Krakow, across the border in Poland. At least in Poland she had gone to a regular school, though not all Polish Roma did. Her Czech cousins had been sent to special schools – Roma children were considered defective and inferior. Her uncle's children could barely read, and not because they were not smart.

No, she was not sad to leave this ugly scrap of wasteland, with its black, foul mud and the Nazi messages spraypainted everywhere by the skinheads who wrecked their homes and beat the Roma with baseball bats. She was not sad to leave this place that was heavy with the memories of the pig men with swastika tattoos who carried her off and hurt her in terrible, private ways among the garbage of a roadside dumping station. Her uncle and his family were sad to see her leave, but there was no choice. The thugs would come back, and they probably had friends.

Rosalia and the man driving went on in silence for a few hours, heading southwest instead of north.

"We're taking the long way to Berlin," she said, just so he would know that she knew.

"You think I'd make this long trip just for you?"

They stopped for the first of the other two girls just west of Plzen. She was waiting in a cheap café. No one was waiting with her, and she cried as she got into the back seat. Rosalia kept her eyes firmly focused out the window and kept her hands deep in her jacket pockets. She did not reach out to comfort the new girl.

She should be strong enough to comfort herself, Rosalia thought, wishing the girl would stop crying.

They picked up a third girl and another man an hour later. The girl got into the back seat. Rosalia refused to move away from the window, so the weeper got the uncomfortable spot in the middle. The man, clearly a friend of the driver, got into the front.

The little car was now full, and they headed for the German border.

The passport check was cursory.

"Welcome to the new open Europe," the driver chuckled, tucking the girls' passports into his pocket after they were waved through by the border guards. The other girls objected but Rosalia didn't care. Her passport was fake, and not even a good fake. She didn't have any real papers.

The car stopped in a small town and the three girls were allowed to stretch their legs and go to the latrine. The men bought them sandwiches and coffee, and they all sat together at an outdoor table, as though they were tourists on a holiday. The weeper – a Czech, who had finally stopped weeping – and the third girl, a Romanian, tried to engage the men in small talk: "Do you go to Germany often?" and "I can't wait to see Berlin on my days off."

Rosalia kept her mouth shut. She listened, and she watched.

She watched the expression on the men's faces as the girls talked, and saw how they wore the sort of face people put on when they're forced to listen to people they don't consider equals. She'd seen that same expression on too many Czech and Polish faces when the Roma tried to talk to them.

She saw the way the men's eyes constantly scanned their surroundings, and recognized in that the eyes of her own people, who could not rest from watching for the police.

And she noticed how little time it took for them to jump up from their seats and come after her when she wandered away for a little walk.

She took all this in, and thought about it as they continued their journey.

They stopped for the night at an ugly cinder-block motel. Everyone went into one room.

"Sleep," the men said, pointing at one of the double beds for the three girls to share. Rosalia kept her day clothes on, even her shoes, and took a space at the bed's edge, refusing to move even when one of the girls asked her to.

One of the men stretched out on the other double bed and was soon snoring, and the other sat up awake in a chair.

Rosalia dozed with one eye open and heard the men change places halfway through the night. She waited until the snoring started up again, and then slowly, quietly slipped out of the covers.

The man in the chair had his eyes closed. He appeared to be sleeping.

Interested only in testing, not in escaping — after all, where would she go? — Rosalia reached for the motel room door. She turned the bolt on the lock and opened the door onto the deep German night.

Slam! The man on watch was out of his chair and smacking the door shut. "Where are you going?"

"For a walk."

"No walk!"

"What's going on?" And then both men were up, standing over her, yelling at her in Romanian and German. "You want to get in trouble — out in Germany without papers? You want to get us in trouble? Damn Gypsies!"

One man raised his arm to strike her.

"Not on the face!" his companion shouted.

And in that instant, Rosalia knew, and she could tell that the men knew that she knew.

The arm returned to the man's side, then came back out in a rush and hit into Rosalia's stomach with such ferocity that she buckled and fell to her knees. He pushed her into the dirty carpet with his foot.

The other two girls were whimpering, arms wrapped around each other, trying to look small on the bed. Rosalia did not cry. She got to her feet and got back in bed, pulling the covers up to her chin.

She closed her eyes, but she could feel the men glaring at her. She heard the bolt lock again, and she heard the chair being pulled into a position right against the door.

"You two – if she gets away, you will both pay," one man said to the girls. "Now, go back to sleep!"

"Take her shoes," the other man said.

She didn't move a muscle as the covers were pulled from under the mattress and her sneakers were untied and yanked off.

"Now try to get away."

Rosalia kept her face still, but inside, she was smiling. As if a lack of shoes could keep her from running.

/ / / / / / /

They were up and in the car again before the sun came up. No one was sleeping anyway, so the men decided they might as well be burning up miles. They sent all three girls into the bathroom together to get ready.

"I'm watching you," the Czech girl cautioned Rosalia. "I'm going to Berlin. I'm not blowing this chance and I'm not going to let you ruin my life."

"Your life is already ruined," Rosalia was tempted to say, but she kept her mouth shut. If the girls couldn't see the signs for themselves, they wouldn't be convinced by anything she had to say.

They made brief stops, no more picnic lunches. A few toilet breaks, sandwiches eaten in the car, the men trading off between driving and sleeping. It was raining. They hadn't returned Rosalia's shoes, and the socks on her feet were wet and cold.

Rosalia read the highway signs and saw they were heading to the northern part of Berlin. The car finally turned into a housing complex beside a big shopping mall. It stopped in the parking lot of a row of short apartment houses.

The men got out quickly and one took a firm hold of Rosalia's arm. She was allowed to carry her own suitcase. The other man kept up cheery patter about how the girls would enjoy shopping at the mall on their days off.

Rosalia kept her eyes open. She saw the name of the street – Zühlsdorfer – and took note of the giant number one painted on the front door.

On the third floor, they stood before apartment 3A. One of the men knocked, and the door was opened.

More men were inside. Rosalia counted four of them.

Six men in total, and three girls.

In spite of herself, she started to tremble.

"This is what you've brought us?" one of them asked. "You travel all that way, and come back with this?"

"Clean them up, they'll be good enough," one of the drivers said. "Keep the lights low."

They saw she had no shoes. "Problems?"

"Too much spirit. We calmed her down."

"We'll see."

Rosalia was taken away into a small room with a narrow bed and a little bureau with four slender drawers. Three of the men entered the room with her and shut the door behind them.

She tried hard to control her shaking, but it had taken over her whole body. She put her suitcase on the floor by the bureau, then stood upright with her shoulders back and her head high.

I am brave, she told herself.

"You're shaking," one of the men said.

"My feet are cold," she replied, in careful but correct German. She was far from fluent, but could manage simple sentences.

She immediately realized she'd made a mistake. It would have been better not to let the men know she could understand them.

"We'd better get you out of those wet socks then," a man said. He bent down to take them off.

"I will do it," she said. She stripped her feet bare of the filthy, wet socks.

Then she coughed a deep chest cough. It was a cough that sounded like a cross between whooping cough and bronchitis, wet and contagious.

The three men backed away.

"You have your own toilet," one said, "through there." And they left her alone.

In case they were watching her through the keyhole, Rosalia kept her face passive as she went into the little room that had just a toilet and a sink. There was a rack with a towel on it. The towel was threadbare, but it was clean, like the rest of her space.

Rosalia washed her socks in the sink, rubbing most of the dirt out with the bar of hand soap, and hung them to dry beside the towel.

She washed herself in the sink and put on track pants for sleeping. Before turning out the light and crawling into bed, she moved the little bureau across the door. The horrible-sounding cough covered up the noise of moving furniture.

She got into bed, for the moment feeling fine.

The cough was fake. Her brothers had taught her. They'd used it to get their mother to bring them hot tea in bed on cold mornings.

Back when their mother was alive. Back when they had beds.

They'd taught her a lot of things. She was a good student.

/ / / / / / /

Early the next morning, Rosalia took a closer look at her surroundings. The window in the small room would not open and was mostly painted over, except for a foot or so at the top that let in a bit of light. By standing on her bed, she could see outside.

The apartment building looked over a large park, still green in the fall, with trees that were starting to change color. Train tracks ran along one side of it, and apartment blocks rose up all around it.

She coughed again while she moved the bureau and got washed and dressed quickly. The apartment was quiet, but she was hungry. Maybe she could get some food and get back into her room before anyone else woke up.

She tried the door but it wouldn't open. She was locked in her room.

She was about to examine the window again – maybe there was a way to unlock it, a way to shimmy down a drainpipe three stories to freedom below – but she heard movement in the outer apartment.

Someone had opened the apartment door. Rosalia heard the jangle of keys, then heard water running, cupboard doors opening and closing, and soon smelled coffee brewing.

Her bedroom door was suddenly unlocked.

"Oh. You girls have arrived, have you? I suppose I'll have to open another jar of jam. How many are you?"

The woman at the door was short, perhaps in her mid-sixties, and she peered at Rosalia with an air of accusation.

"Good morning," Rosalia said in German. She held out her hand. "My name is Rosalia."

"Are you the only one?" The woman ignored the outstretched hand.

"There are two others."

"More work for the same wages," the woman muttered as she turned away, but she left the door open, and Rosalia stepped out.

The apartment was a mess of liquor bottles, plates of old food and cigarette butts. There was no sign of the men, but Rosalia assumed they were asleep somewhere.

The woman kept working in the kitchen, and Rosalia got busy tidying the other room. It could only help her to have this woman on her side.

The woman showed surprise at the tidy living room, but just said, "I guess you'd better come and eat."

Rosalia sat at the kitchen table. She didn't try to make conversation again. She just ate as much as she could hold. There were hard-boiled eggs, dark rye bread, slices of cheese, and jam. She kept eating as the other two girls joined her. Rosalia drank lots of coffee and watched the other girls pick at their food.

Too foolish to know they'll need their strength, she thought.

After breakfast the girls were put back in their rooms. Rosalia asked no questions, but the other girls did, and they got no answers from the housekeeper other than, "I've got my orders." Rosalia used the time to go through the exercises her brothers had taught her, keeping her legs strong with squats and lifts, her arms strong with push-ups and isometrics, and her stomach muscles hard with crunches and twists.

Then she stood back on her bed and looked out the bit of window. She watched cars and trams going by, and she saw people pushing strollers and walking dogs.

She was still standing there when the door was unlocked again, and the housekeeper came in with her broom and cleaning supplies.

"You've made your bed," the woman said. "You're a tidy one. I like that."

Rosalia took that remark as an invitation to chat.

"What is that park?" she asked. She wasn't really interested, but one bit of unimportant information might lead to others, maybe more vital.

"That park? That's Marzahn. This whole area is Marzahn. Metro station's called Marzahn, too, although I don't expect you'll be going on many trips. Are you going to be this tidy every day?"

Rosalia didn't understand all the words — the woman

spoke too quickly — but she got the question and replied, "I like to be tidy."

"Well, I can use the help around here," the woman said before she shut the door and locked it. Rosalia did another round of exercises.

The men got up an hour or so later. Rosalia thought she heard one man walking around, mumbling complaints at the housekeeper. Then other men entered the apartment and talked with him. They left the girls locked in their rooms.

A meal was brought in on a tray and left on the bureau. There was stew, bread and more coffee. Rosalia ate everything quickly, while it was hot.

She had just swiped the stew bowl clean with the last bit of bread when she realized where she was.

She had heard the stories, and the tales must have included the name, but it hadn't stuck in her head, not like the other names and the other places.

Marzahn was the first concentration camp for Gypsies.

Rosalia pushed aside the tray and stood back up on the bed.

The park, now green and golden, had been the place where the Nazis had gathered together all the Roma and Sinti of Berlin in 1936, and forced them to live in squalor, guarded by dogs and men with guns.

It was the Olympics, the government said. We want Berlin to look good for the world. We want the garbage off our streets.

So they rounded up the Roma people – people like Rosalia's great-grandparents, whose ancestors had lived in Germany since the 1400s – and they kept them prisoners for the crime of being Roma.

Rosalia tried to picture it. She tried to picture the barracks, cold and crowded, and the barbed wire, and the barking dogs, and the shooting guards. Down below, where people now jogged and walked their poodles, her people had suffered.

"So many died of illness," she remembered her grandmother saying. "They died of hunger and the cold. And some died fighting."

The stories came flooding back.

That park out there belonged to her as much as it belonged to anyone in Germany. Her family's blood and tears had fallen on the soil where flowers now grew.

In 1944, the order came to clear the Roma out of Marzahn. The soldiers came to herd the people into trucks and trains. Her great-grandmother had stood with the others in her barracks, clutching bars of iron and boards of wood, and beating the heads of any Nazi soldiers who came near.

The Germans backed down.

"Some of the soldiers were just boys," Rosalia remembered being told. "They didn't know what to do with women who fought back."

The victory hadn't lasted. All the Roma and Sinti of

Marzahn were sent to Auschwitz. Only a handful were still alive at the end of the war. Rosalia's great-grandmother was one of them.

My family are fighters, Rosalia thought, as she heard a knocking on the apartment door and more men came in.

She kept up her fake cough, coughing as close to the door as possible so the men would be sure to hear her.

They left her alone again that night.

She coughed all through the pleading, screaming and crying of the other two girls. She coughed while the parade of men laughed and slapped and grunted and drank. She coughed and thought about her great-grandmother fighting off the Nazis.

She knew she would not be left alone another night.

/ / / / / / /

"Put this on," the housekeeper said, handing her a skimpy dress, spiky high-heels and a plastic container with bits of make-up in it. "I'm to take your other clothes."

She waited while Rosalia put on the dress and shoes, then took her other clothes and her little suitcase. She closed but did not lock the door behind her. Music started to play in the living room. Men entered the apartment.

Rosalia took off the shoes. She stuffed one of them under the bed, then curled her hand around the toe end of the other. She put both hands behind her back. Then she stood and stared at the door, thinking about what had happened at Marzahn before she was born.

The door opened.

"Time to start earning your keep," a man said, and another man came into the room. "Thirty minutes, or you pay more," he was told. Then the door was shut.

"Don't just stand there. You heard him. Tick tock." He was at her in two steps.

"I do not want this," Rosalia said, clearly and in German. She was sure she had the words right. "I am fourteen years old, and I do not want this."

"I was told you were a fighter," the man said, grabbing her shoulders and drawing her toward him. He forced his fat, slimy tongue into her mouth.

Rosalia bit down, hard, and brought her knee up into his groin at the same time. The man folded in pain. She swung the shoe at him, aiming the stiletto at the soft point in his skull. He dropped to the floor.

She waited a moment, catching her breath, to be sure he was unconscious, and to be sure the men outside had not heard him fall over the sound of the music playing. Then she took off his shoes, his pants, his jacket and his shirt. She gathered them all into a bundle, tying them together with his belt, and used the stiletto heel to break through the window. She dropped the clothes outside, slicing her arm open.

She grabbed a chunk of broken glass just as the men came bursting into her room.

Rosalia had cut an artery, and the blood spurted out in a gush. She flung it at the men, hitting some of them in the eyes.

Waving the broken glass, she leapt through the men, slashing out at anything in her way, and made it to the apartment door.

She had trouble with the locks. There were too many.

"Let me out!" she screamed at the housekeeper, who was standing with a tray of drinks. The men were coming after her.

The housekeeper didn't move. A man was almost at her, almost grabbing her.

Rosalia turned quickly, jagged bloody glass pointing out. She stabbed the man hard in the belly, leaving the glass shank inside him.

She got the last lock undone and flung the door open. She bolted down the stairs, leaping two and three steps at a time.

Down she ran, around and around, leaving a trail of blood, willing herself not to get dizzy, willing herself to stay upright. There was the front door, and then she was out on the street.

Bloody, barefoot, and in a dress too skimpy for the chilly fall night, Rosalia took a big breath of free air. She found the bundle of clothes in some shrubs, then dashed across the parking lot.

Through families of shoppers coming out from the mall,

around moving cars, narrowly missing trashcans, Rosalia ran. With the bundle tucked under her armpit, she kept one hand clamped firmly over her wound. She heard one shoe then the other drop out of her bundle as she ran.

She was at the point of collapse, but she could not stop now. The park was dark. If she could just get there, she could find a place to hide. Probably, they were following her. She didn't take the time to turn around and check.

Steps up took her over the train tracks, and steps down took her to the laneway that led to the park. As she got closer, she could see that the park was really a cemetery, and that it was closed for the night.

The low fence at the entrance was not going to stop her. The bundle went over first. She had to unclasp her wound before pulling herself over. It was almost impossible, but the shadows in the park were waiting for her. She had to get there.

Then she was over, and after a few steps more she reached the deep shadows and bushes. She collapsed in a thicket of trees.

Rosalia undid the bundle and wrapped the shirt around the wound in her arm, using her teeth to help her tie it tight. She put the trousers on over the foolish excuse for a dress and pulled the jacket over her shoulders. There wasn't much she could do about her bare feet, but cold feet were a small price to pay for freedom.

She sat hidden in the trees and the shadows, peering out

at the cemetery entrance and the laneway leading to it. No one was coming after her, or at least no one had chased her into the park.

Rosalia put her hands in the trouser pockets to keep them warm. In one pocket was a wallet, and she could feel the edge of bills folded inside it. She found some keys, which she tossed into the trees, and some coins. Just inside the cemetery entrance was a pay phone. She knew what she had to do.

She left the comfort of the shadows and made her way to the telephone. She dropped several coins through the slot and pressed some numbers.

"Fire!" she yelled, using the German word, and she gave the address of the apartment. "Children! Hurry!" She didn't think anyone would come if she just said girls were in trouble. Then she hung up and went back to the shadows.

She found a spot by the fence where she could look across the train tracks and see the apartment building where she'd been held. It wasn't long before she heard the sirens and saw the flashing lights of the police and fire trucks.

Maybe now the other two girls would be rescued. Deportation or even prison would be better than what they were going through in that apartment.

And now the fatigue really set in. She knew it would be better to keep running, to put as much distance as she could between herself and those men, but she was too weary. She moved deeper into the cemetery, with its quiet paths and comforting darkness.

Just beyond the area of German headstones she came upon a sign. *Sinti und Roma.* An arrow pointed the way. She walked in that direction.

Light filtered in from the pole lights above the train tracks. Rosalia stepped into a large square of grass full of low stone nameplates.

She bent down to touch a stone and could just make out the name:

Irina Sajetz, born 19-2-1920, died 31-12-1943

She moved to another one.

Hanna Srasko, born 10-5-1878, died 30-1-1944

There were more, many more — the Roma and Sinti who had died in Marzahn concentration camp and the German citizens who had stood up to the Nazis, also sent here to eventually die.

She sat among the markers. This may have been the very spot where her great-grandmother had beaten back the Nazi soldiers.

Rosalia raked her fingers along the grass and thought about that fight.

How scared her grandmother must have been! And how brave!

A bit of sparkle caught her eye. Tiny black stones surrounded the base of a memorial statue. Rosalia picked up a handful of the shiny marble pieces and held them in her hand. She folded her fingers and held the jagged stones tightly, so that the edges pressed into her palm.

All the people who had been brought to this camp had wanted to live. They wanted to laugh and love and be with their families. They didn't want to be treated like garbage. They didn't want to go up in smoke.

And they didn't want to give up.

She wouldn't give up, either.

The man's wallet in her pocket had money in it. She was healthy, brave and strong. She had a better chance than most, and she was not going to throw it away.

Rosalia opened her hand, looked at the bits of marble, then looked back at the grave markers of her people. She put the marble pieces into her pocket. She'd keep them always, then pass them on to her own child, if she ever had one. It was almost like having a piece of land.

She left the graveyard, climbing back over the fence, and found the entrance to the metro station. A couple of Euros fed into a machine got her a ticket. There was a map of Berlin nailed to a wall.

She'd go to the station that was the farthest west.

Germany was not a place for her to stay. France was

next, then England. She'd find somewhere. The world was a big place. She'd find a home.

The train came into the platform and she got on. The train car was heated and its floor was kind to her bare feet. She'd find shoes somewhere, but first she wanted to get away.

She picked up a discarded newspaper, kept her head down and headed out on the next part of her journey.

ELEVEN

A cushion hit Abdul on the head, waking him up.

He jumped to his feet and found himself standing toe to toe with a glaring Rosalia.

"Keep away from me," she said.

"I wasn't bothering you."

"You were watching me sleep. I will throw you off the boat."

Rosalia snatched up the little bag of black pebbles, stuffed it in her trouser pocket and stomped away.

"I wasn't bothering you!" he called after her. She cursed back at him in three languages from the other end of the boat.

"She's really angry."

Abdul heard Jonah's voice.

"I'm up here."

Jonah was sitting on the roof of the wheelhouse.

"Be careful up there." Abdul said, as he climbed up and sat beside him.

"You sound like my mum. She was always saying things like that."

"That's what mothers do. When did she die?"

"I was eight. She died just before Christmas. Happy Christmas to me."

"Was she sick?"

"She took a lot of drugs."

"Oh."

"Is your mum waiting for you in England?" Jonah asked.

"No. She's dead."

"Your dad?"

"He's dead, too."

"So you're alone then?"

"I guess I am."

"Why are you going to England?" Jonah asked. "England's nothing special, but people always want to go there."

"There's something I have to do."

"Like a job?"

"Isn't that why most people go to England?"

"Maybe you don't need a job," said Jonah. "Maybe you're already rich. You never paid my uncle."

"No. I didn't."

"So you owe him. But he's dead. So now you owe me."

Abdul laughed.

"You want me to pay you? That's not going to happen."

"You owe me," Jonah said. "If you don't want to pay me money, you could just...take care of me."

"Take care of you?"

"We'd take care of each other," Jonah said quickly. "I'm a hard worker. I could make your tea and run to the take-away."

"Find someone else. I'm no good at taking care of people. Ask Rosalia. Ask Cheslav."

"Cheslav doesn't like me," said Jonah. "And I'm afraid of Rosalia. So that leaves you."

"No. It doesn't. England is your country. People there will take care of you."

"Strangers."

"I'm a stranger, too," said Abdul. "And I'm hungry. Do you want to help me make supper for everyone?"

"No! I don't want to help you. And I don't want to live with you, either. I can take care of myself!"

"Jonah..."

"Go away. I don't even want to sit with you." Jonah turned his back to Abdul. "My uncle was right. You're just a dirty Arab."

The words hit Abdul like a slap. He climbed down from the roof and left the boy alone.

Rosalia was in the wheelhouse at the controls.

"I'm taking us out of here," she said, turning on the motor.

"Jonah's on the roof."

Rosalia yelled at Jonah to get down so he wouldn't fall when the boat started to move. Jonah did as she said but went to the farthest place he could go on the deck and kept his back to them all.

"Who started the boat?" Cheslav came into the wheelhouse.

"I want to get to England," Rosalia said. "England is north. I'm taking us north."

"We could pass England and go straight into the North Sea," said Cheslav. "If we go straight west we will go out into the Atlantic Ocean."

"Northwest, then," said Abdul. "If we miss England, we'll hit Ireland."

"Northwest," Rosalia decided. "I will do this. You will back away and stop crowding me."

Cheslav took a step toward her, but Abdul took his arm and led him out of the wheelhouse. He'd had enough of people being angry for one day.

////////

Down in the boat's tiny kitchen, Abdul opened cupboard doors and slammed them so hard they bounced open again.

"I am so sick of these people!" He took down a bag of macaroni noodles and a can of tuna. "I'll make a hot meal for myself. I don't care if they starve."

He turned to fill a pot with water and saw Cheslav leaning in the doorway.

Abdul felt foolish for talking out loud, even though he'd been speaking in Kurdish and doubted Cheslav could understand him.

"Do you eat tuna in Russia?" he asked in English.

"In Russia, we eat caviar."

Abdul laughed. He found the can opener. He could feel the Russian's eyes on him. Cheslav was watching him the way his younger cousins watched him back in Iraq.

"If you're going to watch, you might as well work." He handed over the opener and the tuna and turned his attention to the noodles. He emptied them into the boiling water and turned to see Cheslav holding the can opener, a look of confusion on his face.

Abdul took it back, stuck it into the tuna can and gave the handle a couple of turns. Then he handed it all back to Cheslav. The utensil was awkward in the Russian's hands but, after a couple of turns, the can was open.

Abdul strained the tuna into the sink. After a while he fished a couple of noodles out of the pot, tried one to see if it was done and handed the other to Cheslav. Cheslav chewed carefully, then nodded. Abdul poured the noodles into a strainer, shook the water out of them and put them back in the pot on the stove with the heat off.

"My father taught me to cook," he said. "He liked to give my mother time to paint when she wasn't at her job."

"Someone always cooked for me," said Cheslav.

"Your mother?"

"No!"

"Then who?"

"They cooked. They didn't talk."

Abdul let it go. He added the tuna and some butter to the noodles, then handed a wooden spoon to Cheslav.

"Stir," he said.

Cheslav stirred.

They divided the supper among four bowls and took them up on the deck. Jonah was still in a bad mood and refused to join them in the wheelhouse. Cheslav said he'd be happy to eat Jonah's share, and Jonah came in and ate.

After supper, Abdul took a turn at the wheel. Everyone stayed together in the wheelhouse. No one talked, but at least, Abdul thought, they weren't fighting. He suspected that they, like him, were thinking ahead to the next stage of the journey. Once they landed in England, they would go their separate ways. He couldn't say he was actually friends with Cheslav and Rosalia, but they weren't enemies, either. He wasn't really looking forward to being alone.

Though it won't be for long, he reminded himself. One last thing to do, then no more worries. No more loneliness.

"I'll clean up," Jonah said. He gathered up all the empty bowls. "See? I can work hard." He went below.

"What did he mean?" Cheslav asked.

"He wanted me to look after him in England," Abdul said. "I told him no."

"He's old enough to look after himself," said Cheslav. He left the wheelhouse and went below.

"The English will look after Jonah," Rosalia said. "They would not let you be with him even if you wanted to."

"He says I owe him because I still have the money I didn't give his uncle."

"That's right," said Rosalia. "You still have money."

"Do you have people in England? I mean…" He hadn't meant to do this, but now he couldn't see any way not to. "I mean, if you don't have any money, I could let you have some of mine."

"In exchange for what?"

"For nothing. You could just have it. Because we are traveling together."

"We are not traveling together." She got up and stood at the wheel to look into his face. "We are all alone on this boat. I am alone. The boy is alone. You are alone. The Russian is alone. You have some idea that we are friends, but we're not."

"Fine." Abdul stepped away from the wheel so Rosalia could take over. He headed out of the wheelhouse, then turned back. "I don't know what happened to you, but you have no right to accuse me of wanting to hurt you. I don't know you, but you don't know me, either."

Abdul went to the back of the boat and watched the

water churn up from the motor. He could not wait to get to England and get away from these people!

He tried to calm himself. He curled his toes the way his father had taught him. As always, it helped.

He put the others out of his mind and tried to picture England so he could be prepared. It was hard to make a plan without knowing what he was heading into.

England would be orderly. That much he knew from the photos he had seen in books. The British liked stone walls, neat pathways and traffic laws. There would be hedges and street signs and little shops that never ran out of things.

It would make the most sense to look for a dark place to land the boat, so that meant countryside or a small town. Abdul wished he knew how much he would stand out. He knew there were people who looked like him in England's cities, but would he be too much of a stranger in the countryside? Would people see him and call the police?

After he got rid of Jonah, he would be free. Maybe there was a train or a bus he could catch, but that idea made him feel cooped up and trapped. If someone tried to come after him on a train or a bus, he wouldn't be able to get away.

It would be better to walk. It would take him longer, but time didn't mean much anymore. He'd walk at night, hide during the day and eventually, finally, he would get to his destination.

His fingers went to the thin chain around his neck and he absentmindedly rubbed the medallion.

He could spend his money in England. He could go into a store and buy food. He could even buy a way out of the rain – a cup of coffee in a restaurant, a ticket to a cinema. If he was careful, the money he had would be all he needed.

Abdul heard a sound behind him. Cheslav pushed a blanket-wrapped bundle ahead of him out of the entrance to the stairs.

"I cleaned out the cupboards," he said. "I'm going to sell all this in England." He took a screwdriver from the boat's tool kit and began to remove a brass bell that was screwed to the boat.

"How are you going to move around with all that?" Abdul asked. "Won't it slow you down?"

"I am not worried about that." The bell clanged as he put it into the bundle, tied the ends of the blanket together and straightened up.

The smile on his face changed to a look of alarm.

"Lights!" he shouted. "Coming this way! We are being chased!"

He ran to the wheelhouse and shoved Rosalia away from the wheel. Abdul fell to the deck as the boat jolted forward at full speed.

"I'm not getting caught!" Cheslav yelled. He aimed the boat toward a bank of thick fog. "I'm not going back! I'm not going back!"

TWELVE

"I don't know what I'm going to do with him."

The housemother looked down at Cheslav, standing between two policemen.

"It's the third time he's run away, and he's only been with us for two years."

Cheslav stood on the front step of the Baby House, wet from the rain he'd been running in. He was too tired now to try to escape the grip of the officer's hands on his arms.

"He's not too big to tie to the bed," one of the officers said.

"I don't like to do that with the older ones," the housemother said. "At least he's nearly seven. Soon he'll be someone else's problem."

The police officers handed Cheslav over to the housemother and left. Cheslav was marched up the stairs and down the hallway to the room where the older boys slept.

"No more outings for you," the housemother said. "Get your pajamas on."

Cheslav's fingers were numb with cold. He had trouble undoing the buttons. The housemother, impatient, yanked his shirt over his head.

"You won't find your mother by running around Cheremkhova. Now I have to wash these clothes. You are nothing but work."

She left the dormitory. Cheslav heard the click of the door locking behind her.

He stood in the middle of the room and shivered. The dorm was cold and he was chilled from the rain. Whispers of children rose up around him.

"Chicken got caught! Chicken got caught!"

That's what they called Cheslav. Chicken. Because he was scrawny and bony and spent playtime running along the Baby House fence looking for a way out, just like the chickens the housemother kept.

"Chicken got caught!"

Someone threw a pillow at him. He picked it up and went to his mat — one of twenty that took up most of the floor space.

There was no blanket on his mattress. Another child had taken it. Cheslav curled up around the pillow to try to get warm.

"That's mine," said the boy who had thrown the pillow.

Cheslav clutched the other boy's pillow closer to his chest. He wrapped his arms around it and held tight.

"Give it back."

The other child started to tug. Cheslav heard the sound of feet running across the floor as boys left their mats to crowd around and watch. Several joined in trying to get the pillow back.

Cheslav was kicked and hit but he held fast to the pillow. His eyes were shut. He entwined his fingers together even as the boys tried to pry them apart. For long minutes, he took their abuse.

Then, in a flash, he was on his feet and swinging. The other boy's pillow flew out of his hands. But it was no longer about that. It was about hitting what he could hit. It was about getting relief from the rage that had built up inside him.

"What's going on in here?"

The dormitory door flung open. A shaft of light flooded in from the hallway.

"You again!"

Cheslav was lifted out of the middle of the fray by the housemother's strong arms. She carried him out of the dorm.

"I've had enough." She tossed him into the supply closet and locked him in the dark.

Cheslav jumped and roared and clawed at his surroundings. Everything he could reach he yanked down from the shelves and threw against the walls. The blankets fell to the floor. The bars of soap and cleaning supplies ricocheted off the walls, often hitting him in the head but he didn't stop.

He threw himself over and over against the locked door.

Finally, he fell to the floor in exhaustion. He made himself a nest in the blankets. And slept.

/ / / / / / / /

"What about this one?"

The housemother brought Cheslav forward. A tall man in a military uniform peered down at him.

"He doesn't look big enough," the man said. "We don't take boys before they're seven."

"Cheslav just turned seven," the housemother said. "He's small but he's strong. I think he's just what you're looking for."

"What are these marks on his head?"

Cheslav still had scars from things landing on him in the closet.

"Playground injuries," the housemother said. "You know how boys are."

The uniformed man was all sharp corners and straight lines, all shiny brass buttons and dangling medals. He bent at the waist to look at Cheslav more closely.

"Cheslav, is it? I'm the dean of the junior school at the Siberian Military Academy. Step forward, boy. Let's see how strong you are."

Cheslav didn't like being stared at, but the man made him hold out his arms and keep his head high.

"Nice straight back," the man said. "Parents?" he asked the housemother.

"Father dead in a mining accident just after Cheslav was born. His mother found herself an Australian husband and left the country."

"She's coming back for me," Cheslav said.

"I'm sure she is," the man said. "And when she does, she'll be proud to see her little boy standing tall like a man, all smart and polished in a cadet uniform. What do you say? Would you like to come to my academy?"

The man was smiling. He looked right at Cheslav as if Cheslav's opinion mattered very much.

"My mother won't be able to find me if I leave."

"We'll leave your new address with the housemother here. You don't want to stay at the Baby House forever." The man raised himself up to speak with the housemother.

"We'll take him right away," he said. "Best not to give him too much time to think about it."

Cheslav was bundled into the dean's car that very morning, his few belongings packed into an old Aeroflot shoulder bag.

"You be nice to everybody," the housemother said as she waved goodbye. "Then everybody will be nice to you."

The academy was a few hours' drive from the Baby House, on the outskirts of Irkutsk.

"You look like a brave boy," the dean said to Cheslav as they pulled into the grounds of the Siberian Military Academy.

"You probably don't cry much. Am I right about that?"

Cheslav nodded. He cried at night sometimes, but the man probably couldn't know that.

"Good for you. Here's a piece of advice. Don't let the other boys see you cry. Ever. They will make fun of you, and I want you to enjoy your time at my academy. I was a student here, and they were the best years of my life. Do you think you can do that? Enjoy yourself and learn?"

"My mother will be able to find me?"

The dean sighed. "She'll find you."

"Then I will learn."

Inside the academy, Cheslav was handed over to his dormitory master, a boy named Gregor from the ninth form. Gregor took him to his dormitory.

"This is where you will sleep," he said.

They stood in the doorway of a long, narrow room. Cheslav stared at the row of bunk beds lined up so close to each other that there was just a narrow space to walk between them. The walls were white. The blankets on the beds were gray.

Gregor took Cheslav down the row of beds until they came to one with a bare mattress. The sheets and blanket were in a folded pile at one end.

"Looks like you're stuck with a bottom bunk," Gregor said. "But that means it will be easier to make up your bed."

He started to unfold the first sheet. Cheslav stood back, watching.

"Do I look like a housemother?" Gregor asked. "You have to make your own bed and keep your space clean. Everyone does. I'll show you this time, but you'd better pay attention because if you do it wrong, you'll be in trouble."

Cheslav didn't want trouble, so he watched and helped and tried to learn.

Against the other wall were small cupboards.

"Keep your clothes in here," Gregor said. "Keep them folded. You're in the army now, and we keep things tidy in the army."

Cheslav put the Aeroflot bag in the cupboard.

"Unpack it," ordered Gregor. "Then hand over the bag. You won't need it again. You're not going anywhere."

Cheslav's personal belongings were few. He had an old pipe that had belonged to his father, which Gregor took away because pipes were not allowed. He had an old biscuit tin that held odd rocks, plastic animals, a few marbles and a tiny metal car. And he had a glossy magazine.

"You're a little young for this," Gregor said, snatching it away. "Whoa – look at them!"

The magazine was full of photographs of beautiful women dressed in nice clothes.

"There's only one thing to do with women like this," Gregor said, and he made kissing noises at the photographs.

"That's mine!" Cheslav tried to snatch it back. "My mother is in there!"

Gregor looked at the magazine's cover.

"*Russian Brides for Elite Gentlemen.* Your mother is one of these women? Show me." He handed the magazine back to Cheslav.

Cheslav knew the spot. He found the photo easily but he had to bite the inside of his cheek to keep from crying at the sight of his mother's face smiling out at him.

"'Ivana Petrovka, 29, MA in Pharmacy Studies, likes to sew, cook and dance. Her ideal man likes fun, adventure and a happy home.'" Gregor laughed as he read the caption under the photo. "Your mother is a mail-order bride. Did she land a rich German?"

"Australian. And she's coming back for me."

"You'd better study hard in English class, then."

Gregor put the magazine in Cheslav's cupboard and closed the door. He took Cheslav to the quartermaster and left him there to be kitted out in his new uniform.

After getting dressed in his navy trousers, white shirt and navy jacket, it was time for lunch.

In the Baby House, he'd had his special seat at one of the low tables in the playroom. The housemother or one of her helpers would bring him his food on a tray. When he was done they'd take the tray away and wipe his face and hands with a wet cloth.

The academy had a dining room. No one had a special seat.

At his first meal, Cheslav got in line with the other boys, all looking alike in their dark blue uniforms but all different in size. There was a lot of pushing and butting in.

"Don't just stand there — pick up a tray!" Cheslav was told when he found himself in front of a stack of trays.

He had to push the tray along a counter he couldn't see over. A series of ladies in hairnets put things on it — a plate of stew, a piece of bread, a slice of cake, a glass of milk.

From the food line it was a short walk into the large dining room. It was hard for Cheslav to carry his tray, watch that nothing spilled and keep an eye out for an empty space at a table.

"New boy."

Cheslav saw a blue uniform step in front of him. He stopped and looked up.

It was a much older boy, from the senior school.

"New boy, can I have your piece of cake?" the older boy asked.

Cheslav remembered what his housemother had told him, to be nice.

"Okay," he said. The older boy took his cake.

"New boy." Another boy spoke up. "Can I have your glass of milk?"

The boys around them started to laugh.

"Okay," said Cheslav. The milk was taken, drunk, and the empty glass replaced on the tray.

Cheslav took a few more steps.

"New boy! Can I have your bread?" This one didn't wait for an answer. He just took the bread.

By now the whole dining room was quiet and watching.

"Oh, new boy," came another voice in a sing-song, mocking tone. "Can I have your stew?"

Cheslav looked up at the smirk on the older boy's face and the meanness in his eyes. The boy was twice his height and had a thick neck below a large head.

He nodded. A hand reached out and took the plate of stew.

The boys in the dining room started to laugh. Then a chant rose from the tables.

"Cry! Cry! Cry! Cry!"

It went on.

Somehow, Cheslav managed to carry his tray to an empty spot at a table. Gregor was there.

"You didn't cry," Gregor said. "That's something. Do you want some of my lunch?"

Cheslav wasn't hungry. "Will they do this again?"

"They don't usually stop until you cry."

It happened again at supper. And it happened the next day at breakfast. Cheslav did not cry when he saw his food disappearing, but he was growing very hungry.

At lunch the second day, he got to the dining room in time to see the older boys reduce one of the other new boys to a crying heap on the floor.

The chant changed from "Cry! Cry! Cry!" to "Baby! Baby! Baby!"

Cheslav got in line, picked up his tray, got his portion of

noodle casserole and sliced fruit, then began to walk into the dining room.

"Ah, here he is, and just in time, too. I'm extra hungry today!"

The older boy stood in Cheslav's way. "I'm tired of doing this bit by bit, new boy. Today, I want all your lunch."

Cheslav was seven, and small. The tray was a little bit heavy for him, and awkward to carry.

It wasn't something he'd thought about before this moment, but somehow his hands knew what to do. They knew how to keep the tray balanced while they changed position. And they knew how to lift it up, turn it, and in one quick, fluid motion, smash it into the other boy's belly.

Afterwards, he didn't run away. He stood still as the tray clattered to the linoleum and watched the noodle casserole fall off the older boy's uniform.

There was silence in the dining hall.

Then the older boy, soaked with food, picked up Cheslav by an arm and a leg and, with a guttural roar, flung him across the room.

Boys ducked and fled as Cheslav flew through the air. He landed on a table-top and bounced onto the floor.

"Are you hurt?" Gregor asked as he helped him to his feet.

Cheslav kept his mouth shut. He concentrated on the

pain in his knees and back. By thinking about it really hard, he kept himself from crying.

When supper time came, Cheslav got his tray. It was stew again, chicken this time, with dumplings. His body was bruised and aching and he shook as he carried his food.

The older boy stepped in his way again.

"You think you've won the war, don't you?" He bent down to look Cheslav in the eye. "You haven't even been to a battle yet. Yeah, I'll leave you alone. There are easier kids to pick on. But there are people like me everywhere. You got that? Everywhere."

"Hey, you want to wear the new boy's dinner again?" the older boy's friends laughed.

The older boy moved in closer and whispered in Cheslav's ear.

"You'll never be safe from us."

Gregor steered Cheslav to a table far away from the pack of older boys.

"I don't want to stay here," Cheslav said.

"Where else are you going to go?" asked Gregor.

"Australia."

"Forget about your mother," Gregor said. "This is a good school. You'll learn all about how to be a soldier."

"What if I don't want to be a soldier?"

"Everybody wants to be a soldier," Gregor said. "Go ahead. Eat. I'll watch your back."

Cheslav stopped shaking. He looked down at the food on his tray, then started to eat. He ate everything on his plate. He was very hungry.

///////

His life settled into a routine. At the academy, everyone was kept busy all day long. They did a lot of military things, even Cheslav's young class. They marched around the yard with pieces of wood shaped like rifles angled smartly at their shoulders. They stood at attention when the Russian flag was raised. Some of the boys in the class had trouble standing still or sorting out their left foot from their right. Cheslav didn't. He watched what the older kids did and he did the same. It made him feel grown-up.

The students were assigned jobs according to their age. Cheslav's class had to dust all the baseboards in the hallways every day. One of the senior boys lined them up in two rows, spread them down the length of the hall and got them to work. The organizing took longer than the dusting.

Cheslav didn't mind the chore, but he did mind how some of the older students would walk down the hall, see the little kids on their hands and knees and shove them to the floor by stepping on their backs. The older students called this "playing dominoes."

It happened three times to Cheslav.

The fourth time he heard the older kids start to flatten his classmates, he waited, head down, until it was almost his turn.

Then he wrapped his arms around the bigger kid's legs and brought him crashing to the floor. Blood from the older student's nose spattered onto the linoleum.

Cheslav heard a lot of yelling and felt himself being kicked like a football from one side of the hall to the other. He smashed hard into the walls. His head buzzed with the impact.

Strong arms lifted him up by his ankles and he was carried upside down out of the school building. He was dumped face first into the pile of snow on the edge of the assembly yard.

Cheslav heard his tormentors go back inside the school. He raised him himself up, brushed the snow off his uniform and face and started walking across the frozen field toward the woods.

He almost made it there before the headmaster looked up from his paperwork, saw him through the window and sent someone running after him.

Cheslav spent a week in the infirmary recovering from the cough he got after being out in the cold.

He didn't tell the headmaster who had given him the bruises. He sat in silence and refused to answer any questions.

There were no more games of dominoes. And when the older boys saw Cheslav in the hall or in the exercise yard, they would say, "Stay away from him. That one is crazy."

Having the others think he was crazy meant that no one picked on him anymore. It also meant that no one wanted to be his friend. When he moved up to form two, and tried to warn the new group of seven-year-olds about the thugs in the dining hall, they seemed more afraid of him than of the older boys.

It didn't help that he showed up at every weekly mail call looking for a letter from his mother, each time walking away empty handed. Others would get cards from family and even parcels full of treats. Once a boy took pity on Cheslav and gave him a bar of chocolate his aunt had sent. Cheslav flew into a rage and threw the chocolate into his face. The boy got a black eye. Cheslav spent an afternoon in the Brig, a bare room with a door that locked.

No one shared their parcels with him after that.

"Cheslav is a problem," he overheard one day while he was sitting in the reception room outside the headmaster's office. He was nearly eleven. Soon it would be time for him to move from the junior school to the more serious senior school. "He has a bad temper. We are here to train officers. We cannot have officers who cannot control themselves."

"He's a smart boy," said another man. Cheslav recognized the voice of his form four teacher.

"Based on what? His academic scores are only average. He can drill but he shows no potential for leadership."

"He's had a rough start," the fourth form teacher said.

"But his arithmetic scores are not bad. And he tries hard in English-language class."

"That's the only class he tries hard in," said the physical training master. "He has no team spirit. Doesn't care whether his team wins or not. He's fine on the individual challenges — swimming and the obstacle course. He's small for his age but well-coordinated. But the other boys don't like him. No one wants to partner with him for judo and he's always the last to be chosen for any team. They think he's crazy."

"Will he do any better in any other school?" the form four teacher asked. "The Russian army is big. He will find a place in it."

Soon after, Cheslav was called in. He saluted and stood at attention before the headmaster's desk.

"You have been moved up to the senior school," was all that was said, but just as Cheslav was leaving the office, his fourth form teacher whispered, "Congratulations."

Marching became more serious in the senior school. They did close-order drill for an hour each day, in double rows of ten, carrying real rifles. They learned to make sharp corners and execute commands in an instant.

"You could be sloppy as children," the drill instructor said. "We expect a higher standard from you now that you will soon be men."

They shot at targets with real ammunition, did war games in the forest and were drilled in basic first-aid.

Cheslav stopped showing up at mail call. He was too old to be waiting for his mother to write to him. And when another student went into his cupboard and stole the catalogue with her picture in it, he didn't complain. She was a stranger to him now.

Then, in the second month of his first term at the senior school, he was told to report to the music room.

"Your form four teacher says you're smart," the music master said to Cheslav. "I could use a smart student in the band. Pick out an instrument and let's see what you can do."

Cheslav walked slowly down the row of instruments. The saxophone had all those holes and knobs, as did the clarinet and the flute. They looked too complicated.

The fourth instrument in the row was a trumpet. It had only three buttons.

Only three, thought Cheslav. He picked it up. It felt right in his hand.

"Playing the trumpet is as much about vibration as it is about notes," the teacher said, showing him how to place his fingers, how to shape his mouth.

The first sounds were terrible.

"Take it into a booth," the teacher suggested. "Try it out."

The music room had five small soundproofed booths. Cheslav went into one and closed the door. He tried again to make a sound, and again it was awful.

He started to despair.

Finally he turned his back to the door, stood right in the back corner, squished his eyes shut and put the trumpet to his mouth once more.

The sound that came out was sweet and clear.

Startled, he almost dropped the instrument. Then he tried again.

It worked better when his eyes were closed, when he could block out the world around him and just feel the music as it came out.

He played around with notes, with pressure, and with breath. He played at the mouthpiece with his tongue, changing the pitch almost just by thinking about it.

He stood with his eyes closed, playing with these new sounds, until he felt a soft tap on his shoulder.

Reluctantly, he opened his eyes.

The music was gone, and he was back in the gray practice room.

"The dinner bell has gone," the teacher said. "Come back again tomorrow."

Cheslav handed over the trumpet without a word and floated to the mess hall. He didn't notice until later that evening how much his facial muscles hurt. The ache made him smile.

"I've got a trumpet face," he said to his dorm-mates.

"You've got an ugly face," they said back, and looked relieved when he just smiled.

He went back to the music room the next day, skipping breakfast. He played in the practice booth with his eyes shut until he felt the tap on his shoulder.

"You'd better learn how to read music," the teacher said.

Cheslav worked hard at it. The first time he followed the notes and out came a recognizable tune, he felt so happy he was sure he could float right up over the academy.

They put him in the marching band, and that was okay, because he could march and he could play, but his trumpet sounded better when his eyes were closed. They put him on stage with the senior band to play for Founders' Day and graduation.

When Cheslav was thirteen, the Founders' Day ceremony was attended by important men in the Russian military. A new missile factory was opening in their area, and a general stopped at the school after inspecting the factory.

"We live in a time of Russian strength," the general said in his speech to the students. "I envy all of you being young and coming into the army at this great time in our history." He talked for a long time, but Cheslav, sitting with the band, was not listening. His eyes were closed, and he was listening to how his first solo in front of the school would sound.

Finally the general stopped talking and Cheslav took his spot in the center of the stage. He waited until the music teacher nodded, then raised the trumpet and closed his eyes.

He played a piece by Tchaikovsky, a piece usually played by a whole orchestra, but he played it all with just his trumpet. With his eyes closed, he could see the notes, feel the crescendos and inhabit the music as it inhabited his trumpet.

The applause was jarring to him. He would have preferred silence so that the music could fade slowly away, but he took his bow as he'd been trained and went back to his seat with the band.

Later that day, he was summoned to the headmaster's office. He sat in the reception room and listened to the voices coming from the inner office.

"A talent like that can't be stuck in this backwater."

"Irkutsk is a vital part of the nation."

"I have already made the calls. You act like this is an injustice."

"He's happy here."

"The decision's been made."

Cheslav was called in. He made a salute and stood at attention before the headmaster's desk.

"You've been given a great opportunity," the headmaster said. "You are being transferred to the Army Cadet Music School in Moscow."

"There are fine musicians there like yourself, and you will learn from them and be a credit to Russia," the general said.

"Can't it wait until the boy is sixteen?" the music

teacher asked. "Sixteen is the age for cadets."

"Special circumstances," the general said. "Have him ready to go first thing tomorrow morning. He'll fly back to Moscow with me. The defense minister is attending our next company assembly. I'll present the boy then."

Cheslav was dismissed. He skipped the evening snack and sat on his bunk. He didn't know how to feel.

In the morning he was bundled along with the general and staff into a military plane. The general let him have a window seat. He slept most of the way and missed seeing Russia from the air.

The academy of music was in a large building of yellow stone, part of a complex of military buildings on an army base a little way from the center of the city.

Cheslav was the youngest student and the smallest.

"We'll need a doll uniform for you," the cadet in charge of the clothing supply said. "You got any dolly uniforms back there?" he called to his assistant.

The smallest uniform was handed to Cheslav, and even then he had to turn up the cuffs.

"We'll have that," the head boy in his dorm said, sweeping away the dark blue uniform of Cheslav's old school. "If you run away, we'll want to know what color to tell the police to look for. It's army green now for you, dolly."

The barracks at the music academy was much like the dormitory at his old academy in Irkutsk, although he now had a foot locker instead of a cupboard. The sounds that came from the boys were louder and deeper. The sounds of men, backed up by the muscles of men. Muscles that shoved Cheslav away from the sinks in the lavatory and slammed him into the gravel of the exercise yard.

"We worked hard to get here, dolly," he was told again and again. "What have you done?" and, "This is an army for men, dolly, not little girls."

It didn't help that he'd joined the school months into the new term. And it didn't help that the older cadet assigned to show him the ropes was embarrassed to have Cheslav in his company and lied to get out of his duty. Cheslav was forever getting lost, arriving late and breaking rules he didn't know existed.

The first company assembly was held a week after he arrived. The general was there to introduce his discovery to the school and to the honored guest, the minister of defense.

The whole academy was assembled in the Great Hall. On stage was the First Tier Band – the band that was reserved for the most talented senior students. Cheslav was backstage, running through some scales to warm up.

It felt wonderful to have a trumpet back in his hands. He hadn't been able to hold one since coming to Moscow. The general had ordered him to keep his talent a secret so that everyone would be overwhelmed at his debut.

The First Tier Band had completed its number and the general started to speak.

"We will finish off this assembly with a special treat. I am about to bring out a boy I discovered in an academy in Irkutsk. He is our newest cadet, a boy of extraordinary talent. He is living proof that the Russian people are great, even in the most far-flung corners of the Motherland."

"So, *that's* your friend, is it, dolly?" whispered the cadet in charge of pulling back the curtain. "You're the general's dolly? Better fix your tie before you go out there."

Cheslav put down the trumpet and went to the small mirror at the side of the stage to make sure his uniform tie was straight. Then he picked up the trumpet again and stood ready to go on.

The cadet opened the curtain and gave Cheslav a rough push that had him tripping his way onto the stage in his too-large uniform. A bit of laughter came from the audience.

Cheslav didn't care. He stood alone in the middle of the stage and raised the trumpet to his lips. But when he took a breath and started to play, no sound came out.

The snickering grew louder. Cheslav raised the trumpet again and took another deep breath. He put his lips to the mouthpiece, but again, no sound came out.

He looked inside the trumpet. In the short moment he had put it down to straighten his tie, someone had stuffed his horn with putty or chewing gum.

The laughter from the audience didn't matter. The anger on the general's face didn't matter. All that mattered was that someone had interfered with his ability to make music.

His body began to shake. He flung the damaged trumpet far out into the audience, ran back to the band and grabbed the first trumpet he saw from one of the band members.

Back on the center of the stage, Cheslav planted his feet, raised the trumpet in front of him and blasted out "Flight of the Bumblebees" by Rimsky-Korsakov — as loud and as angry as he could make it.

Not a sound could be heard when he finished playing. Cheslav remained on the center of the stage, holding the trumpet. A tall cadet with a trombone in his hand took his arm and led him offstage, through the halls and into the music room. He closed the door.

"My name is Kolya," the cadet said. "Have you ever heard jazz?"

And then Kolya lifted his trombone and started to play.

A whole new world opened up for Cheslav.

During the day it was marches by Borodin and Kozlovsky. But at night it was Miles Davis, Dizzy Gillespie and Louis Armstrong.

There were six cadets in an informal jazz group. They were all seniors except for Cheslav. The age difference disappeared when they played music.

"Throwing your trumpet was a very jazz thing to do," the older boys told him. "Jazz is about making your own rules. It's about feeling things and living by the off-beat, not marching in step."

Their days were so full of classes and military training it was hard to find the time to play. Or a place.

They were thrown out of the mess hall when they tried to play jazz during their lunch break. They were banned from playing jazz in the senior boys' common room, and when they tried to play outside on good days, they were told it interfered with close-order drill.

"You have not been brought here to waste your time playing such music," the headmaster told them when they were all summoned to his office. "You are corrupting our youngest student. I order you to stop."

Cheslav was forbidden to associate with them. He did it anyway, and walked punishment tours back and forth across the assembly yard.

One night, Cheslav was awakened in his dorm by Kolya, who pressed a hand over his mouth to keep him from crying out in surprise. Throwing on a sweater over his pajamas, he followed Kolya through the quiet halls to the music room. The clarinet player had stolen the music master's key. They all crowded into one of the soundproof practice booths and played until first light came through the music room windows.

After that, they played jazz together every night. Cheslav stayed awake until the other boys in his barracks were quiet before sneaking out to the music room.

He often fell asleep in class. He didn't care.

"We need to go to America," Kolya said. "We should all go to New York or New Orleans or Chicago. These are cities that appreciate jazz. We will get jobs playing the right kind of music. And we won't have to sneak around as though we were criminals."

"Let's go now," Cheslav said. "Let's leave right away."

"Oh, we are going to go," they all said. "We will leave Russia behind and cross the sea to the United States. What good lives we will have!"

"I'm ready," Cheslav said.

Every night they talked about their plans. They talked about how they would steal things from the school and sell them at pawnshops to raise the money for their trip. They talked about the vodka they would drink, the women they would get and the music they would make. And every night Cheslav said he was ready to go.

Until one night a cadet from his dorm followed him down to the music room and brought a prefect with him.

The music academy had a brig just like the academy in Irkutsk, only this one was larger and cadets had to stay there longer.

Cheslav was given a punishment of two days for being out of his barracks after hours. It took six senior cadets to get him into the cell and shut the door.

"We will put your bad behavior behind us now," the headmaster said when Cheslav was brought before him after serving his punishment. "The older boys have been a bad influence on you, but you have an incredible talent. With proper guidance you will grow to be a true credit to Russia."

"What about Kolya and the others?"

"They will no longer bother you. There is a great need for new young officers in Chechnya. You can be proud of them. They are on their way to becoming heroes."

Cheslav tried to leave that night but his dorm-mates stopped him.

"We've been ordered to watch you," they said. "We'll be in trouble if you leave."

"I don't care about you," Cheslav said.

"Then care about this." A fist went into his stomach.

Night after night it was the same thing. Cheslav showed up at each flag raising with fresh bruises. Finally the music master had him placed in the infirmary. He was afraid Cheslav's face would be injured and he wouldn't be able to play the trumpet.

"I'll make you a deal," the music master said. "You stop trying to leave and I'll let you play any kind of music you want when there is no one else in the music room."

"I don't want to stay here," Cheslav said.

"You are a cadet," his teacher reminded him. "The school is in charge of you. If you leave, the police will bring you back. So it would be better for you if you learn to like it."

The music master kept his word and let Cheslav play jazz and rock solos when the music room was empty. Cheslav shut himself up in a practice booth, turned off the lights, shut his eyes and played. He missed the others, but it helped him get through the days.

He moved back to the dorm. The other boys were ordered to leave him alone.

Three months after the jazz band left the academy, it was announced at the morning gathering that Kolya had been killed by a sniper while on patrol in Chechnya.

The academy flag was lowered to half-mast and a memorial service was held in the assembly hall. Everyone wore full-dress uniform.

After Kolya's name was entered into the Book of Honor, joining the other graduates who had been killed in battle, Cheslav stood up to play.

He'd been assigned to play Chesnokov's "Keep Peace in Our Souls." When that was done, he was supposed to return to his seat and the assembly would be dismissed.

Instead, when the piece was finished, he kept his trumpet raised and blasted out "When the Saints Go Marching In."

A cadet in the rhythm section was the first to join in, then two from the brasses and a few of the woodwinds. Kolya had been their friend, too. They let Cheslav play the lead and when he took them off into dazzling flights of improvisation, they backed him up solidly.

That night, Cheslav put a spare pair of socks in his jacket pocket, grabbed his trumpet and walked away from the school.

He headed west, walking as far as he could. He stole food from street vendors and traveled by night, avoiding the police. He stole civilian clothes off a clothesline and buried his cadet uniform in a forest. He crossed the border into Belarus hidden in the back of a truck that took him all the way to Minsk.

By the time he got to Stuttgart, he hadn't eaten for four days.

He found a pawnshop and walked inside.

"How much?" Cheslav held out the trumpet.

"No good." The pawnshop owner pointed out all the marks and dents on the trumpet. It had been well used at the school and had traveled roughly with Cheslav.

He slapped fifty Euros down on the counter.

"More," said Cheslav.

"You steal it?"

"No!"

"Identification." The pawnshop owner held out his hand.

"Never mind," said Cheslav. "I want my trumpet back."

"My trumpet now," the shop owner said. "Go ahead. Call the police."

Cheslav threw himself at the pawnbroker, but the man was ready. One punch landed Cheslav on the floor. Before he could get to his feet, the pawnbroker picked him up and shoved him out the door, locking it behind him.

Cheslav yelled and rattled the bars that covered the glass.

A police car drove by.

He backed away. He felt bitter and hollow inside.

His mood had not improved by the time he got to Calais.

THIRTEEN

The yacht inched along in the darkness and the fog. Abdul had no idea where they were, if they were closer to shore or farther away from it. He stood at the front of the boat and kept watch.

The fog started to lift as the wind came up, and daylight found the boat rising and falling in big rolling waves.

"Are we heading northwest again?" Abdul asked Cheslav, popping his head into the wheelhouse on his way to the kitchen to make more tea.

"Unless you've changed your mind and would rather go back to France."

Abdul left him to it and went below to put water on to boil. He thought about changing into dry clothes, but decided that could wait until they got to England. Surely it couldn't be long now.

It was tough keeping his balance on the rocking boat while carrying a tray of tea things, but he managed, only spilling a little. Rosalia, keeping watch at the front of the boat, lowered the binoculars and accepted a mug, along with a slapped-together sandwich of cheese and bread.

"Thanks," she said.

"You're welcome. Long night."

"Long journey."

"I hope it's almost over."

Rosalia nodded toward the sky. Dark storm clouds were sitting like boulders in front of them.

"It's going to be rough," she said, after swallowing a mouthful of bread and tea.

"We have a bigger boat now," Abdul said. "It won't be like last time."

He finished his tea, collected the cups and took everything below. Then he got out the lifejackets. He put his on first, then took one out to Rosalia. She put hers on without an argument. He woke up Jonah and helped him into a vest, securing the straps for him.

"Put this on," he said to Cheslav.

"You think I can't swim? You wear two if you're scared."

Abdul put his hands on the wheel. "There's a storm coming. I'm not having you end up like the Uzbek. You are going to put this on or I am going to put it on you. You'll probably beat me bloody in the process, but you will end up wearing it."

Cheslav relented. "Just to save you a beating." He put on the life vest and fastened it.

"I think I see land!" Rosalia called out.

It took a moment. The swell of the sea had increased, and Abdul had to wait for the right balance of rise and fall and the right clearance of a fog patch, but then he saw it.

Land. Unmistakably, land.

His fingers rose to the thin chain around his neck, to be sure it was still there.

"It's England," he said.

"Or Greenland. Or Newfoundland," said Cheslav. "Or maybe we've sailed right through the Beaufort Sea and are looking at Siberia." But he sounded cheerful. "I'll take us in."

Certain there were things that should be done on a boat before a storm, Abdul tried to figure out what those things would be. He made sure the portholes were closed and locked tight. He crammed anything that was loose in the kitchen into cupboards and secured those. And he shoved Cheslav's parcel of treasures back down the stairs, along with his own bundle of spare clothes, a bag of things Rosalia was taking and Jonah's old clothes, now clean and dry. Then he secured the staircase door.

The wind was getting stronger and the waves were getting bigger. They made the yacht rise high, then drop like an elevator.

He saw Jonah on the back deck, gathering cushions off the benches. The wind blew him flat to the floor. Abdul made his way over to the boy by clutching anything nailed down.

"Get into the wheelhouse," he yelled.

"I want to help."

"You're too small. You'll end up in the water."

"I'm not useless!"

"I didn't say you're useless. I said you're small."

"I can — "

"Be quiet!"

A sound reached Abdul's ears through the roar of the sea and wind. It was a sound that was far too familiar.

"Listen!"

Then Jonah heard it, too, and then they all saw it.

A helicopter, coming closer and closer. It got close enough for Abdul to see its red belly and read the word "Coastguard" on its side.

"What is a helicopter doing out in this storm?" Rosalia asked.

"Maybe they're looking for us."

"What should we do?" Jonah asked.

"Go faster," Abdul yelled.

The boat gave another lurch as Cheslav ramped up the speed. Jonah was thrown back onto the wet deck. A dip in the waves sent him sliding to the other side of the boat. His hands flailed about as he tried to find something to grip onto, but there was nothing. He slipped through the railing.

Abdul could see Jonah's hand clutching the base of the railing, white-knuckled. With a great yell, Abdul heaved himself across the slippery deck. Waves of sea-water pushed him back. He dared not take his eyes off Jonah's hand.

He tried again to get to the boy, his eyes stinging with salt water until he could no longer see anything but a blur. And then he made contact with someone.

It was Rosalia. She had thrown herself face down on the deck and was gripping the railing, reaching through the smacking waves to get a hold on Jonah. Abdul held onto her until he could get his own grasp on the railing. He shoved his free arm out the side of the boat and attached his hand to Jonah's arm, the one arm that was keeping Jonah with them.

Jonah was still hanging on, but the swaying of the boat bounced him and knocked him hard against the hull.

On his own, Abdul would not have been able to do it. Jonah would have slipped through his hands and into the water, and then they would have lost him forever.

But Rosalia was there, and the two of them grabbed whatever parts of Jonah they could get a grip on, and pulled. Bit by bit, and then in one final yank, they got him back up through the railing and into their arms.

They slithered along the deck with Jonah still face down into the shelter of the wheelhouse.

Jonah cried out in pain when they turned him frontside up.

His face was a bloody mess. His nose had been knocked

hard against the side of the boat. Abdul couldn't tell if it was broken.

A bigger cry came when they tried to move his arm.

The noise of the helicopter drove Abdul crazy. He went back out on deck just as a flash of lightning struck like a spear into the sea, followed by a huge bang of thunder.

"Get out of here!" Abdul yelled. "We're just a bunch of worthless kids! Get out of here!"

The helicopter lifted up and away. Abdul knew the pilot hadn't heard him, that it was the storm that sent it away, but he couldn't help feeling a sliver of victory.

Now all they had to do was find a safe place to land the boat.

FOURTEEN

"How is he?"

Abdul knelt down beside Cheslav as the Russian tended to Jonah with bandages and dressings from the yacht's first-aid kit. Jonah's face was smeared with blood, but the nosebleed was over.

"I don't think anything's broken," Cheslav said. "His shoulder is sprained, but I don't think it's dislocated." He placed a sling on Jonah's arm and motioned for Abdul to lift and support the boy while he wrapped and tied the sling in place.

"Where did you learn to do that?" Abdul asked. The bandages on Jonah were tight and neat.

"I used to be in military school. They taught us how to tear people apart and how to patch them back up again. Help me lift him."

Together they lifted Jonah onto the padded bench and wedged him there with cushions against the rocking of the boat.

"I'm sorry," said Jonah.

"Why are you apologizing?" Cheslav asked. "You must be an idiot." He gently washed the blood off the boy's face and Abdul covered him with a blanket.

"Can I do anything?" Abdul asked Rosalia at the wheel. "Do you need a break?"

She turned the wheel over to him.

"Just for a little while. My arms are sore from keeping the wheel straight."

Within a few minutes Abdul knew what she was talking about. All the muscles in his arms, neck and back started to ache from the tension of trying to keep the boat steady. At times it felt like the waves were pushing them forward. At other times it felt as though the waves were pulling them farther out to sea. And when the sea wasn't pushing them closer or pulling them farther from the shore, it was rocking them violently from side to side.

At least England was getting closer. Abdul could see the coastline now without the binoculars — land rising where the water stopped.

It looked like ordinary land. After all his travels, he wondered why he expected more. Greece did not have Athena and Zeus drinking ouzo in the olive groves. There was no reason to suppose the shore of England would be anything other than what it was — shades of gray against a storm-gray sky.

The world was all pretty much the same. People lived

in deserts or forests or cities, but it was all land. He knew in his brain that England would be no different.

But with his first real, naked-eye look at it, Abdul realized he'd been hoping for something more.

He'd been hoping for Lennon and McCartney to be sitting on a dock, playing their guitars, an empty chair beside them. And he would put his feet on British territory, walk toward them and sit down in the chair. And then John — never mind that John was dead — would hand him a guitar, Paul would ask, "What kept you?" and then they'd all get down to writing music.

Although Abdul could now see the shore, he could not imagine what would be there to receive them.

If it's Lennon, he thought, then we've crossed over to a whole other shore.

"My turn," said Cheslav after twenty minutes, and Abdul was glad to let him take over the wheel. He put the binoculars around his neck and scanned the shoreline. All he saw were rocks and cliffs.

"Maybe we should go west for awhile," he suggested. "We can look for a safer place."

Cheslav tapped the fuel gauge. It was almost on Empty.

"No. We go on. While we still have power."

Abdul looked at Rosalia and Jonah. They nodded.

"How do we land in this?"

"You have the binoculars. Find us a place."

The rain started then — not in drops but in buckets.

Sheets of rain so thick it was hard to see through it.

We'll be smashed on the rocks, Abdul thought. The shore was much closer now and it looked even meaner close up.

"Find me somewhere!" Cheslav yelled.

Abdul left the shelter of the wheelhouse and went to the front tip of the boat. He was soaked in a second and had to hold the binoculars with one hand and clutch the railing with the other to keep from toppling into the sea.

He stared so hard that when he finally did see something he was sure he was seeing things.

He wiped the lenses, wiped his face and took another look.

The vision was still there.

Someone in a yellow rain slicker with the hood pulled low was standing atop a high abutment in the cliff, making big arm gestures at them.

Maybe I'm going crazy, Abdul thought. But what choice do we have?

Aping the gestures of the real or imaginary creature in the yellow raincoat, he showed Cheslav which way to go.

The sea and the wind shifted into slow motion in Abdul's mind. He didn't return to the wheelhouse. He was the one leading them into shore. If they were all going to die, it was right that he die first.

He felt calm. He had a plan, and he always felt better when he had a plan. His plan was to be a mirror of the vision in the yellow slicker. When it waved them west, Abdul waved them west. When it waved, "Come straight on," Abdul relayed that to Cheslav.

They were heading straight for a wall of rocks. At any moment the waves would smash them into a cliff and they would all break apart and become debris in the sea.

Not a bad death, Abdul thought. At least we'll die trying. I tried, Kalil. I really tried.

And then he saw what the yellow slicker was trying to get him to see.

There was a channel coming up between the rocks. It wasn't a wide channel, and because the cliffs all looked alike it was hard to see, especially in the storm. But it was there, directly below where the slicker wearer was standing, and the slicker's arms were pointing down.

"In here! In here!" the arms were saying.

Abdul staggered quickly back into the wheelhouse.

"There's a way," he told Cheslav. "Go straight. There's an opening. It's all right. I think we're all right!"

Then, back out on deck, Abdul let the binoculars hang from their strap. He needed both hands to direct. A little to the left — now more to the right. Then they were right in the channel, and Cheslav could see for himself.

The waves rushed in and were sucked back out to the open sea. But as they moved farther in and rounded a bend, they found themselves in a hidden cove, the water a bit calmer and the wind held back.

Abdul started to look for a place where he could secure the boat, and then he saw the yellow slicker again, running down the rocky cliff like a mountain goat.

"Over here!" it gestured.

The yellow slicker jumped up and down as the boat came into rope-tossing distance. Abdul threw, and the slicker secured it to a boulder that looked as though God had created it just for that purpose.

They needed to get the boat closer to the shore so that they could get off. Right now there was a deep, wide chasm between their deck and the rock platform. The creature in the slicker – which Abdul could now see was a child – was trying to pull the rope to bring the boat closer but didn't have the strength.

Rosalia grabbed the rope that was fastened to the back of the boat. She climbed over the railing and held on tight until the waves pushed the boat close enough for her to jump to shore. Then she helped the child secure the ropes.

Cheslav and Abdul went into the wheelhouse and helped Jonah off the boat.

The child led them to a small cave carved out of the rocky cliff. Abdul and Cheslav had to duck down to fit through the low opening, but then they could straighten up and take in their surroundings.

The darkness of the cave gave way to soft shadows, then to brighter spots as the child struck matches and lit candles.

"Is this England?" Abdul asked.

"It's Cornwall." The child shook back the hood of the slicker and revealed the face of a girl around eight, framed by two long braids. She was wearing a school uniform. "Some people think it's the best part of England."

The cave had a narrow mattress neatly made up with blankets. Abdul and Cheslav steered Jonah to it.

"You'll get the bed wet and then it will be no good," the girl said. "Put him on the floor and dry him off first."

The floor of the cave was covered by an old piece of broadloom and a dozen scatter mats. The girl quickly pulled several of the mats together and they gently helped Jonah to sit down on them.

"I'll get some dry clothes," Abdul offered, although he hated to go back onto the boat, even for a minute, now that he was finally in England. But he needed to get dry, too. They all did.

He paused long enough on the boat to put a pot of water on to boil, then gathered up an armload of blankets, towels and dry trousers and sweaters.

"I'm not changing in front of girls," Jonah said as Cheslav untied his sling.

Rosalia looked at the girl. "What is your name?"

"Gemma."

"Gemma, you will come with me to the boat and I will change clothes there." She rummaged through the things Abdul had brought until she found something to wear. Then she led Gemma out.

/ / / / / / /

Dry clothes, warm blankets, hot tea and England. For the moment, Abdul was content.

He looked around the little cave. Cheslav lounged in a lime-green beanbag chair. Rosalia and Gemma shared the mattress with Jonah, and Abdul sat on a seat from an old car.

Colorful pillows were everywhere. More color came from little toys and plastic figurines placed in the nooks of the cave walls. The room glowed warmly from candles stuck into bowls. Wooden crates held comic books and paperbacks and supported plank shelves full of shells, rocks, bits of glass and other gifts from the sea. There were several dolls, too, mangled and with limbs or heads missing.

"I found them on the beach," Gemma said. "The sea always leaves good things after a storm. That's why I'm out here. I'm supposed to be in school, but I didn't want to waste the storm."

"You saved our lives."

"My father was a lifeboat volunteer," Gemma said. "He died in a storm like this. A long time ago."

"My father died, too," Abdul said. "What about your mother?"

"Mum helped me fix up my cave. It used to be my brother's, but he got killed by a drunk driver, so now it's mine."

"Do a lot of people know about it?" Abdul was trying to figure out how safe they were. He'd like to stay and rest up before starting his long walk north.

"Why would I tell anybody? This is my secret place."

"Well, it's beautiful," Rosalia said.

"The helicopter will come back," Cheslav said.

"It might not," said Abdul.

"The Coastguard helicopter?" Gemma asked. "Oh, they come here all the time. They work with the police. A lot of people try to smuggle in drugs around here. You're not drug smugglers, are you?"

The others laughed a little.

"No," said Abdul. "We're not."

"So who are you, then?"

"We're just people who wanted to come to England."

Gemma turned to Jonah. "But you're British."

"Yes. And these are my friends."

Gemma looked each of them in the face, then made up her mind.

"You can't be criminals. You're still children."

"We're not children!" Cheslav objected.

"Well, you're not grownups, and you have to be one or the other." She glanced at the alarm clock ticking on the shelf by the broken dolls. "I have to go. I've got lunch-time detention. They get really mad if you skip that. The village is just across the field. Does he need a doctor?"

"No," said Jonah.

"We'll take care of him," Abdul said.

"All right." Gemma did up the buttons on her slicker. "Will you be here for awhile?"

"For a little while," Abdul told her. "Is that all right?"

"Secret friends in a secret cave. That's all right with me."

She left the cave. Abdul followed her and watched as she scrambled up the rocky pathway to the top of the cliff.

"Thank you," he called after her. She paused, grinned and waved, then disappeared.

"The rain has stopped," he reported back. "What are we going to do about the boat?"

"We leave it there or send it back out to the sea," Cheslav said.

"Or, we could just sink it," said Rosalia.

None of them had ever sunk a boat before.

They began by taking everything off the yacht that they wanted to keep. They took the long bench cushions that Gemma could use in her cave, a box of food and dishes from the kitchen and the big bundle of things Cheslav wanted to sell.

Jonah tried his best to help, but his shoulder hurt too much. Abdul gave him the job of finding places in the cave for the things they carried in.

There was an ax on board as part of the safety equipment. Abdul took off his shoes, rolled up his trouser legs and started swinging at the hull. Cheslav and Rosalia opened the portholes.

It took several swings to smash through the fiberglass. Water spewed in. Abdul moved to another spot and chopped a hole there, too. When he got tired, he passed the ax to Cheslav and then to Rosalia. They kept it up until the water coming in was at their knees. Then they returned to the rocky ledge.

"Come and watch," Abdul called to Jonah.

The four of them stood together and watched as the yacht sank lower and lower. It took a while. The water came up from below, covered the deck and flooded the wheelhouse. And then the whole boat was gone.

FIFTEEN

Everyone started to relax. They made a meal out of crackers and cheese from the box of food taken off the boat. The comic books were passed around. They talked about Spiderman and Wonder Woman. Jonah read out loud to Rosalia. Abdul listened while he explored Gemma's collections.

It was peaceful, picking up the rocks and bits of driftwood, feeling their surfaces worn smooth by the sea. There were shells of all kinds — some the size and shape of his ears, some long and thin like his fingers, some round like his eyes.

One by one, everyone drifted off to sleep.

A few hours later, Abdul awoke with a start. He'd been dreaming that the security police from Calais had tracked him to the cave and were about to beat him. The dream had been so real that he had to leave the cave and breathe some fresh air.

The night was cool and clear. The sea was calm. The storm was over.

He went back inside. Cheslav stirred and opened his eyes.

"What's going on?"

"I'm going into the village," Abdul whispered. "I want to see where we are."

"I'll come with you."

Abdul was glad. He didn't really want to go alone.

Rocks made a natural staircase out of the cove. Abdul and Cheslav climbed up, taking their time in the dark. At the top of the cliff the breeze was fresh. The sky was full of moonlight.

Cheslav and Abdul were alone on the cliff. There was no one else around. A short string of house lights sparkled on the other side of the field.

"Race you," Cheslav said, and the two of them took off, crossing the field in wild leaps like young deer, filling their lungs and pumping their blood full of good air. Abdul couldn't remember the last time he'd run like that without being chased. It felt so good to move his legs full out, to take giant steps on solid ground, to stretch until his legs ached.

They ran together, sometimes Cheslav a bit ahead, sometimes Abdul. They reached the outskirts of the village at the same time. They sat on the gravestones of an old cemetery, catching their breath before moving silently into the empty streets. The clock in the tower of the town hall said two o'clock.

It felt to Abdul like they were walking in a postcard town with a bakery, a charity shop, an old age home, a pub, a couple of churches and a café that promised the best fish and chips in England. He could smell the lingering scent of grease and vinegar.

They stopped in front of a bulletin board and read the town news. The local Shakespearean company was doing an evening called Sonnets and Grog. Someone had lost a black cat named Tinkerbell, and the Naughty Knitters were looking for donations of wool for their Socks for the Homeless program.

They walked into a little park and sat on the base of the war memorial there. They listened to the quiet.

"We're in England," Abdul said, after a time. His voice barely broke a whisper. "We made it. Do you think it's all like this? When the town wakes up, will it still be nice?"

Cheslav pointed to some graffiti scrawled on the base of the memorial.

"There's your answer."

PAKI GO HOME

Beside it was a swastika.

Without a word, they left the park.

They passed through a street full of homes. Most of the houses were dark, the families inside sound asleep. One house had a light on and the curtains open. A mother was holding a small child in her arms, rocking and soothing it. The two boys stood in the darkness and watched until the baby was comforted to sleep and the light was put out.

Maybe that's a home for Jonah, Abdul thought.

They walked back through the town. They were passing the charity shop when Cheslav stopped and stared in the window.

Among the shoes, china and purses in the display case, there was a trumpet.

"Do you want something?" Abdul asked. "I have some British pounds. Maybe we can come back tomorrow and buy it."

Cheslav looked at Abdul. He looked at the trumpet. Then he took a few steps back, grabbed a trash can from the curb and hurled it through the shop window.

He grabbed the trumpet.

Abdul found himself running before he even had time to make the decision to run. They sped through the streets, through the cemetery and across the dark field.

He was so mad when they got back to the cave that he shoved Cheslav right to the ground.

"You could have gotten us both arrested!" he shouted. "I come all this way, and you could have landed me in jail! I said I'd buy you what you wanted. Couldn't you have waited?"

Cheslav folded his arms around the trumpet. He looked up at Abdul and said, "I've waited long enough."

SIXTEEN

When Abdul opened his eyes the next morning, the first thing he saw was Cheslav. The Russian was sitting cross-legged on the other side of the cave, the stolen trumpet in his lap. He was polishing it with his shirt-tail, making the brass sparkle in the candlelight.

"He doesn't even care," Abdul said to Rosalia. "Look at him. He doesn't care that he put us all in danger."

"If you feel you are in danger around me, feel free to go somewhere else," Cheslav said calmly. "I'll be staying around until tonight."

"That's when I was planning to leave!" Abdul sat up and rummaged through the food box to see if there was any juice left. "Why don't you leave this morning? You've told us how much you'll blend in here. You and that stupid trumpet could just walk out of here into the open arms of the British people."

"Stupid trumpet? You are an idiot."

"Shut up, both of you," Rosalia said.

"I know why you think this is stupid," Cheslav said, holding the trumpet up in the air. "You've probably never lost anything that meant something to you."

"Who do you think you're talking to?" Abdul's voice was low, like the warning growl of a dog about to attack.

"I am talking to a boy who is mad at me because I take control of my life, while you spend your days rubbing some little gold disk you have hanging around your neck. Is that your good luck charm? I make my own luck."

"Stop talking." Abdul clenched his fists.

"Let's see this magic necklace." Cheslav crossed the cave in a couple of steps and put his hands on Abdul's shoulders.

Abdul knocked Cheslav to the ground and rolled on top of him, swinging and yelling. Cheslav fought back and tried to grab Abdul's medallion.

Rosalia moved the lit candles out of the way.

"Come, Jonah," she said. "Let's let them kill each other."

But before Jonah could get to his feet, Cheslav and Abdul rolled into him, smashing against his hurt arm. He cried out.

The fighting stopped.

At the same time, Gemma appeared in the doorway.

"Good morning," she said brightly. "I brought breakfast. Are you fighting?"

"It's over," Rosalia said. "They're boys."

Abdul straightened himself up and brushed off his clothes. Cheslav adjusted Jonah's sling.

Gemma took buns and jam out of her school bag.

"Won't your mother miss this food?" Abdul asked. "You didn't tell her about us, did you?"

"I couldn't tell her about you without telling her I'd missed school, could I? And she won't miss the buns. She knows I have a big appetite."

Abdul and Cheslav eyed each other warily as they sat down to eat, Cheslav cradling the trumpet again.

Abdul watched Gemma setting up their breakfast as if she was setting up a party for her dolls. Her school uniform was clean, her hair shiny. She was loved and cared for. She would never be able to understand his life.

Maybe I should just leave, Abdul thought, as he chewed on a roll. Maybe I shouldn't wait until dark. If he started walking now, he could do twenty kilometers or more before the sun set. And if he kept walking through the night, he would really be well on his way by this time tomorrow.

He looked at the change of clothes he'd bundled up for himself, on the floor near the crate of comic books. It would be easy to pick it up and walk out. Cheslav and Rosalia would be left with the problem of Jonah.

He was halfway to his feet when a very angry woman appeared in the entrance to the cave. She was wearing a jacket over a nurse's uniform.

"Hands on your heads, all of you," she ordered. "On your heads or I'll shoot. I'll shoot you dead."

"Mum!" Gemma went to the woman and took her hand out of her pocket where she was pretending it was a gun. "It's all right!"

"What part is all right? The part where I get called at work because you are missing school again? The part where you are sitting with a bunch of strange teenagers who ought to be in school themselves? Or the part where someone broke the charity shop window last night and stole a trumpet?"

She looked at Cheslav. He just grinned.

"And who is this child?" Gemma's mother went over to Jonah. "Which one of you hurt him? What's your name, son?"

Jonah didn't answer.

"Who are you all? Where are your parents? Gemma, start talking."

"These are my friends."

"Your friends. What else? What about you?" she asked Rosalia. "Are these boys bothering you? Do you want to get away from them?"

"I'm all right," Rosalia replied. "I am in no danger from them."

"They're not criminals," said Gemma.

"I suspect at least one of them is." Gemma's mother stared at Cheslav again. "That's it. I'm going to the police. Gemma, let's go."

Abdul stood up. "Please, your daughter is right. We are

not criminals. And I would like to pay for the window that was broken." He undid the safety pins on his trouser pocket and took out his roll of money. "The boy with the sling is Jonah. He's a British citizen and his parents are dead."

"Shut up!" yelled Jonah.

"We would appreciate it very much if you could get him to a doctor, just to make sure he is not badly injured."

"I don't need a doctor!"

Abdul put his money in the woman's hand. "This is all we have. Use it for the broken window and for Jonah."

"Did you steal this?"

"I worked for it. In Iraq. Take it, please. The money was to get me to England. I'm here now. Take it."

"I will pay for my own actions," Cheslav said. He got his bundle and dropped it at the woman's feet. "There are good things in here. Expensive things."

"Stolen things?"

"The men who owned them were going to kill me. Why should I not take their things?"

Gemma's mother took a deep breath. She put Abdul's money in her pocket.

"I work as a nurse's aide at the retirement home. The doctor will be going through there today on rounds. I'll get him to see Jonah. I take it he's not on National Health?"

"He had an uncle," Abdul said, "but he wasn't the sort of man to look after things like that."

"Right. Well, we'll figure it out. Come on, son, before

my boss realizes I'm not in the break room drinking coffee."

"I want to stay here," Jonah said. "My shoulder is fine."

"Fine or not, now that I know about you, I can't just leave you here. On your feet or I'll pick you up and carry you."

"She can do it, too," Gemma said. "She's always lifting old ladies on and off the commode."

"I'm not going," Jonah said. "They'll leave me!"

"Your friends won't go anywhere until they see you again and know you're all right," the woman said. "Tell him."

"We'll wait," Cheslav said.

"Yes," said Rosalia. "We'll wait for you."

"I don't believe you." He looked at Abdul.

I should have left when I had the chance, Abdul thought. I should have just walked away.

He lifted the chain from around his neck and put it around Jonah's.

"I want it back," he said.

Jonah touched the medallion with his fingertips.

"I'm sorry I called you a dirty Arab." With that, he settled down and allowed himself to be led out of the cave.

"After I take care of Jonah, I expect to be told everything," Gemma's mother called back to them. "Got that? Everything."

SEVENTEEN

Abdul was not going anywhere until he got his medallion back.

"Do you trust the woman?" Cheslav asked. "Maybe I should leave now." He tucked his trumpet under his arm. "I have all I need right here. You two can have what's in my bundle."

"I trust her," said Rosalia.

"Why?"

"Because she asked if I was safe. We promised Jonah we would wait."

In the end they all stayed, sleeping the afternoon away until Gemma returned.

"How is Jonah?" Rosalia asked.

"Jonah is good, he's great. At first Mum couldn't get him to talk. Now she can't get him to stop."

"Where is he?" Abdul asked, thinking about his medallion.

"He's at home. At my house. Mum sent me. You are all to come to supper."

"To supper?" asked Cheslav. "Maybe it's a trap."

"It's not a trap," Gemma laughed. "It's roast chicken!" She bounced up the cliff steps and danced around them as they crossed the field.

Abdul found himself thinking of Fatima. She would be Gemma's age now, he realized.

Gemma's small house was on the edge of the village. Abdul took off his shoes at the front door as they were greeted by warmth and smiles and amazing scents of food.

Jonah was first at the door, his arm in a new sling, and wearing new clothes. He was clean. Abdul spotted the medallion around the boy's neck.

"Are you all right?" he asked.

"It's just a sprain. I told you I didn't need a doctor."

Gemma's mother was next to welcome them.

"Come in. Call me Beth. I don't have enough chairs for everyone so we're eating in here."

"It's an indoor picnic!" said Gemma.

Abdul entered the room and he thought his heart would break.

All the furniture had been pushed down to one end of the room. A big bedsheet was spread out on the floor to hold the meal. Everyone would sit on the floor.

It was like he was back in his mother's house.

He closed his eyes. He could see his brothers jostling for positions, trying to tuck their growing legs out of the way.

He could see his father, taking platters of food from his mother and placing them on the cloth, looks of love and laughter passing between them. And he saw himself at Jonah's age, sitting beside his father, listening to him quote Shakespeare as he made sure his big older sons left enough food for his youngest.

Then Abdul saw a guitar propped up casually against a wall by the window.

And he started to cry.

Gemma's mother – Beth – passed him a box of tissues as though it were a normal, everyday thing to have strange teenaged boys crying in her living room.

"That was my son's," she said lightly about the guitar. She dished out plates of chicken and vegetables and passed them around. "Help yourself to the pickles. Jonah told me a lot, and I confirmed his story by calling a cousin of mine who works with the Coastguard. The Americans were picked up unharmed."

"I told you I was telling the truth," Jonah said with his mouth full.

"Yes, you did. This is what we'll do," said Beth. "We'll eat, then we'll talk, then we'll figure out what to do next. You can probably handle your plate better if you put that trumpet down," she said to Cheslav.

Cheslav held a plate full of food in one hand and the trumpet in the other, looking like a statue searching for balance. He could not make himself release the trumpet.

He put his plate on the cloth and ate from it that way. It looked awkward, but it worked.

"Abdul, before I forget, here's what's left of your money back." Beth handed him a roll of bills. "The window is now fixed. And they only want fifty pounds for the trumpet, so I paid them out of that. Maybe Cheslav will pay you back."

"No problem," said Cheslav. "I have no problems now."

I have money again, Abdul thought, checking to see how much he had left. Even if he split the money with Rosalia and Cheslav, there would still be enough for food and for transportation if the weather was bad. There were no more seas to cross and no more borders in his way.

It's almost over, he realized.

"All right," said Beth, once the main meal was over and cleared away. The cloth was folded up so they could all stretch out their legs. Pots of tea and dishes of bread pudding were brought in. "Cheslav. Can you really play that trumpet, or do you just like to hold it?"

"I can play. I will show you." He got to his feet, lifted the trumpet and began.

He played "Flight of the Bumblebees." The notes came out strong and clear and filled with such joy that the flight of the bees became a dance, and the little room filled with the sound of a million happy bees buzzing around.

Abdul had never heard anything like it. He couldn't believe that someone so difficult as the Russian could create sounds so wondrous.

After he was done, it took awhile for the echo to clear from the room and out of everyone's head.

"Extraordinary," said Gemma's mother. "Who taught you to play like that?"

A look of pain came over Cheslav's face.

"I ran away from the Russian army," he said. "That's where I learned to play. But I will not go back! I will go to America, to New Orleans, where they have good jobs for trumpet players. If you try to send me back to the army I will throw myself off a cliff!"

"Sit down, son," said Beth. "Start at the beginning. You are what? Fifteen? How can you run away from the army at fifteen?"

Cheslav told his story. He told it standing up, as if he was ready to bolt at the first sign of someone trying to send him back to the army.

When he was finished he said, "Now I have a trumpet again. It is not as good as my trumpet from Russia, but it will do for now."

"It will do very well," said Beth. "Who's next? Rosalia? What country are you from?"

"I don't have a country," Rosalia answered. She had taken out Gemma's braids and was trying a new way to arrange the girl's hair. "Some say we came first from India. Some say we came from the devil and should go back to him."

And then she told her story. No one remembered to drink their tea. No one even moved.

She came to the end. Abdul couldn't speak.

"Why did you come to England?" Beth asked. "Why do you want to be here?"

Rosalia shrugged. "It's a place. It's a place that's not where I was. There, it was bad. Here — maybe better?"

"And what do you want?"

Rosalia looked puzzled. "I don't know what you mean."

"I mean, do you want to go to school? What do you want?"

"What do I want?"

"Yes."

"I don't know," she said. "No one ever asked me that before."

"I need a stretch and a fresh cup of tea," said Beth. "Gemma, let's get a start on the dishes while the kettle heats up." She picked up the now cold tea pots and headed for the kitchen, stopping briefly in front of Abdul. "And don't think I've forgotten about you, young man."

Cheslav and Rosalia looked lighter, like they'd each put down a heavy burden. Abdul crossed the room, drawn to the guitar. He touched the top. His finger stroked one of the tuning pegs.

"Do you play?" Cheslav came up beside him.

"No."

"I think you do."

"I don't." Abdul turned away from the guitar and went over to Jonah. "I'll take the medallion back now."

"Can't I keep it?"

"No." He wanted to hit the kid. "It's mine."

"I'll give it back. Before I go to bed."

"I want it now."

"I'm not hurting it."

"What's wrong?" Rosalia said.

"Nothing," said Abdul.

"It has writing on the back, but I can't read it." Jonah showed it to Cheslav and Rosalia.

"It's Arabic," said Cheslav. "What does it say?"

"It says mind your own business!" Abdul wanted to leave, shutting the door behind him, shutting away all these people who were trying to pry into his life where they didn't belong. He wanted to walk away and never think about any of them again.

But he couldn't go without the medallion.

When Gemma and her mother returned with fresh tea, everyone looked at Abdul.

"It's simple," he said. "I am from Iraq. My father and brothers were killed by an American bomb. My mother was shot later by the religious militia. I came here." He raised his cup with shaking hands and took a big swallow, even though the tea burned his mouth and throat.

"And how old are you?" Beth asked.

"Fifteen."

"Your father and brothers died in the initial bombing, in 2003?"

"Soon after."

"And when did your mother die?"

"Two years later. A bit more. She was driving a car and they shot her. I stayed with my uncle but it didn't work out, so I left."

"Anything else?"

"I stabbed a policeman in Calais, but it was an accident. There was a riot. Over food."

"And you don't play guitar," said Cheslav.

"No."

It was Rosalia who took the thin chain and medallion from Jonah and held it out to Abdul. He clasped it but she would not let it go.

"What does the writing say?" she asked.

Abdul hung his head.

"It's a name," he said quietly. "It's Kalil."

EIGHTEEN

The American helicopters were on another patrol the first day Abdul started in at the new school.

It was two weeks after his mother's death. His Uncle Faruk agreed to shell out for school fees so Abdul could enroll, even though it was the middle of term.

Abdul was sitting in algebra class, trying to coax his brain into working the way it used to, when the thump-thump of the helicopter came closer and closer until it was right over the school.

The Iraqis were used to it by now, but that didn't mean they liked it. The young men in Abdul's school jumped up out of their seats and ran outside, Abdul joining them. He certainly wasn't going to be the only one sitting there, looking at the teacher.

Outside in the school yard it was a rock fest – rocks and bricks and pieces of wood – anything the boys could find to throw, they threw. Some of the stones glanced off the chopper but none did any real damage.

The soldiers in the helicopter yelled at the boys to stop, and their teachers tried to corral them back into school, but it wasn't until the machine guns started going off that the students paid any attention. Those not close enough to jump back into the school took shelter wherever they could as the soldiers shot at empty places in the yard.

Abdul jumped behind a slab of concrete left in the schoolyard by the earlier bombing of the neighborhood.

"Not exactly 'Lucy in the Sky with Diamonds,'" said the boy crouching next to him.

Abdul looked at him. "I know you."

"It was not a good day," the boy said. "You had just lost your mother. I'm Kalil."

"They say it gets easier."

"They're lying. It doesn't."

Kalil, fourteen, was a year older than Abdul, but they were both in the same grade. So much of their schooling had been disrupted that very few of the students were in the class they would have been without the war. They discovered they lived just two streets away from each other. Then they discovered that they both wrote songs and played the guitar, and Abdul again had a reason to keep living.

Abdul had taken more formal guitar lessons than Kalil, but Kalil had also studied piano, which made him better able to write down the music they wrote. They learned each other's songs. Abdul's were about the real things he saw around him, about the war and hardships. Kalil wrote about the world he wanted to live in instead of the world that was.

"We should write something funny," Kalil suggested, so they wrote "The Bomb That Lost Its Way," a bouncy little tune about a cruise missile with no sense of direction that ended up taking a nice beach vacation on a deserted island.

They wrote about the people in their neighborhood, like the art teacher who began making false passports when the art school was bombed, and families who tried to make the journey to safety along the dangerous roads out of Iraq. They tried to make things work out better in their songs than they did in real life.

"I wrote this last night," Abdul said before class one morning. They'd taken to bringing their guitars to school so they could play every chance they could get. "It's called 'The Car.'" It was about a magical car that only women could drive. It mowed down anyone who tried to stop them.

"You could get into trouble singing songs like that," said a boy from a more senior class who had joined the group listening to them.

"Don't you like his voice?" Kalil joked.

"Women should not be driving."

"Women should not be doing many things, including marrying jerks like you, but I suppose one of them will be forced to."

The older boy took a step toward them, but Kalil was already on his feet. Abdul still looked like a boy, but Kalil was tall and wiry, already developing the shoulders of a man. Besides that, he was fearless and unpredictable.

"You have been warned," the older boy said as he backed away.

Kalil just laughed and launched into a rousing tune called "Fifty Ways to Fix a Bully."

Sometimes Abdul would come up with a bit of a tune, then Kalil would finish it and they would both write the lyrics. Sometimes the lyrics would come first. Sometimes one of them would write the whole song, and when he played it, the other would say, "Why did you put the chorus there? Stick another verse in first." They listened to lots of music when the electricity came on and scrounged for batteries during the long periods when there was no power.

The closer Abdul got to Kalil, the tenser things got with Uncle Faruk.

"You spend too much time with that boy," Uncle Faruk started saying. "You are too much like your father, all the time with the music and the poetry. Quit dreaming and get to work."

His uncle owned several small shops that sold whatever goods he was able to import. Abdul worked hard for him, to keep the peace and pay for his keep, and it made him feel closer to his father that Uncle Faruk hadn't liked him, either.

Abdul spent as much time as possible at Kalil's house. He and his family were Mandaean Sabian, not Muslim, which was another reason why Faruk didn't like Kalil. His father was a goldsmith. Kalil had two sisters, both younger, and they would giggle and whisper whenever Abdul came over.

"We'll be like Lennon and McCartney," Abdul said. Kalil was already growing his hair long, and Abdul was trying to do the same.

"We'll be even better," said Kalil. "Our songs will be better because they are about real people and real stories." He got very excited and started to bounce on his toes, which was what he did when an idea was too great to sit still with. "Here's what we'll do. We will first collect all the stories here in Iraq – all the stories! And we'll turn them into songs. Then we'll go to another country and do the same thing there. We will keep traveling and collecting stories and at the end of our very long lives we will have the whole world, in music!"

"Is that possible?" Abdul asked. "Can we do such a thing? We would need money, passports, visas."

Kalil shrugged.

"We will figure out how to do things when the time comes. Shall we do it? Are you with me?"

"We'll see everything!" Abdul said, bouncing now, too, because it was impossible not to. "We'll see the rainforests of Brazil, the Sahara Desert, the top of Mount Fuji, the bottom of the sea!"

"We will become the greatest songwriters to ever live!" Abdul stopped bouncing.

"Lennon and McCartney broke up," he said. "They stopped writing together."

"It was the money," Kalil said. "There was too much of it. They got richer and richer and it rotted their brains. That won't happen to us."

"Why not?"

"Because whenever we get more money than we need to get by, we'll give it away. No accountants, no lawyers. Our brains will not rot. We'll never forget that it's the stories that matter, the stories and the music. Let's seal the deal."

Abdul wore a ring that had belonged to his father, a simple silver band. He took it off and gave it to Kalil. Kalil reached up and slipped a thin gold chain from around his neck. From it dangled a small medallion.

"My father made this for me when he realized how much I like the Beatles," he said. On one side of the medallion was an etching of the Yellow Submarine. On the other side was Kalil's name in classical Arabic calligraphy.

Nothing else mattered after that, only the dream. For the dream, Abdul worked long hours in his uncle's store, so long and so hard that his uncle even started to pay him a wage, which he squirreled away for the future. He borrowed books on music theory and studied them far into the night, hunching over a candle flame so he wouldn't disturb the cousins he shared a room with. He and Kalil talked with everyone they met, looking for stories, writing and discarding bad songs, refining and improving the ones that had promise.

Abdul didn't care that Faruk was getting more and more grouchy, even getting his sons to hold Abdul down one night so he could forcibly cut his nephew's hair.

"You want to look like a girl?" Faruk shouted. "Are you my niece or my nephew?"

Abdul just looked at his uncle and smiled, even while he was being slapped. He didn't care. Hair would grow back. And he would soon be gone.

When Abdul was with Kalil, he could forget about everything else – the car bombs, the army raids, the headless bodies that would turn up behind his uncle's shop. The war had taken from him nearly everything that he loved, but the war couldn't touch him when he was thinking about music.

And then Kalil's father was killed.

Maybe it was a political assassination – many Mandaean Sabia were being targeted. Maybe it was a robbery committed by ordinary criminals. By that point in the war there was not much to distinguish the two, and there wasn't much of an investigation. Kalil's father became just one more dead Iraqi.

"My aunt is taking my sisters to the south," Kalil said after the funeral. "It's too dangerous for them here, and there is family in the south – well, distant relatives."

"Are you going with them?" Abdul brushed some of the hair out of Kalil's eyes so he could see his friend's face.

"I was thinking," started Kalil. "Why don't we just leave? I don't want to stay in Iraq. Let's just go. Begin our adventure now instead of waiting until we finish school and are old men of eighteen or twenty."

"Could we?"

"I have some money saved, a little, and I can sell some things to get more money. All we need are our guitars and a satchel to keep our songs in. What do you say?"

Abdul was ready. "Where will we go?"

"We're going to pick up where Lennon and McCartney left off, right? So let's go to where they started. Let's go to Liverpool. To Penny Lane. We'll start our new lives there."

It was decided. They would leave in a few days. Kalil wanted to be sure his sisters got away safely, and they both needed to sell what they could. Abdul had some jewelry that had been his mother's. He sold it for much less than it was worth, but it was money he needed. He added that to the money he'd earned at his uncle's shop.

On the day before they were to leave, they arranged to meet in the vacant lot between their two streets. It had held a house before the bombing, and it was a place where they often met to work on their music.

Abdul got there first. His head was full of England. Soon they'd walk the same streets the Beatles had walked, breathe the same air they had breathed.

He saw Kalil heading toward him, his long hair bouncing with every bounce of Kalil's body. His friend looked strong, excited and very happy. Kalil waved at him, a big smile on his face.

Then came the shouting.

"Fag! Homosexual! Disgrace!" Men with sticks came out of nowhere and swarmed over Kalil, swinging and kicking, hitting and cursing.

Abdul couldn't move. He saw his friend fall to the ground but he couldn't seem to move to rescue him.

Finally, he got his legs going.

"Are you with him? Are you with this fag?" A man wielding a metal bar came at Abdul. Abdul shook his head and backed away.

The men kept swinging — and laughing! — until there was nothing left to swing at. They tossed their weapons into the dirt and spat on Kalil's body.

"Death to homosexuals!" they yelled. "We'll kill them all, and all who help them!" Then they walked away.

A small crowd had gathered. Abdul ran forward. He cradled Kalil's bloodied body in his arms, stroking his long, lovely hair that was now sticky with blood. He cried to Kalil to forgive him.

After awhile, someone took Kalil away. Abdul stayed on the ground. When he finally raised his eyes, he saw Uncle Faruk looking down at him with hatred and disgust. And Abdul knew that, even if he wanted to remain, he no longer had a home in the nation of his birth.

The next morning Abdul sold his guitar to a student at his school. He left Baghdad that same day. He knew he would never return.

///////

"I came to England to leave this little bit of Kalil in Penny Lane," Abdul said.

"And after that?"

Abdul didn't answer.

"There's a National Express coach station in the town just north of us," Beth said. "You can get a bus there for Liverpool." She looked around from face to face, then shook her head. "My daughter comes first. You all seem like good kids, but I could be breaking the law by helping you out. You stole a boat. You snuck into the country illegally. Jonah is different. He's a British citizen, but I still have to report him to Children's Services. I don't know how much I can help the rest of you. I'm a single mother. I have to be careful."

"But, Mum!"

"Gemma, hush. You can all stay here for a few days. It's almost the weekend anyway. I'll get you some proper clothes and try to find out where you can go to get some real help. But what I can offer you is limited."

"It is still more help than anyone else has given," said Rosalia.

"We will not give you trouble," said Cheslav.

Abdul didn't say anything, and the room grew awkwardly silent.

"I didn't know Penny Lane was a real place," said Gemma.

"It is," said Beth. "It's a little street not far from where John Lennon grew up."

"It's also a song," Cheslav said to Abdul, handing him Gemma's brother's guitar. "Play it. I know you know how. Play it."

So, he played it. There was no reason not to. He knew where to put his fingers for the chords as well as he knew where to put his feet when he was walking from one place to the next. And although his voice wobbled a bit at the beginning, he got through the first verse clean and clear.

Everyone joined in. Everyone knew it. And when Cheslav played the song's trumpet solo, he played it so sweet and gentle that for one brief moment, Cheslav, Rosalia and Abdul began to feel that they were no longer alone.

NINETEEN

The tea things were cleared away and the crumbs were swept up. Beth started to talk about hot baths for everyone and wonder where they all would sleep.

"Of course you're not going back to that cave. It's no problem to make room here." She took Gemma to see about sheets and blankets while Cheslav and Rosalia finished off the dinner dishes.

Abdul put on his shoes and walked out of the house.

He went to the cliff above Gemma's cave. There was a rock there, a big boulder, and he climbed up on it and looked out at the sea.

The moon was out. The water sparkled.

He knew he wasn't the first person to sit on this rock and look out over the water. Women had watched the sea waiting for their sons and husbands to return. Farmers looked at the water and wished they could be sailors. Sailors looked at the sea and wished they could remain on land. Broken hearts and lonely souls, problems big and small. Whatever you were going through, the sea had seen it all before.

The rhythm of the waves was constant and comforting. Abdul wished he could just slip down into them, quiet and smooth, and let them gently lap over him forever.

It's too bad, he thought, that drowning was not a quiet way to die. He wouldn't magically float down to the sea and be welcomed into its darkness. First he'd have to leave the rock. Then he'd have to climb down the cliff – jumping from above could result in a broken back but nothing more. The sea would be cold and bitter, not soft and easy, and his body would struggle to stay alive even while his mind was willing something else.

He hadn't put much thought into that part of his plan. There had been too many other details to take care of first, just getting done what he needed to do to make the next step in the journey.

All he knew was that once he finished with Penny Lane, he would have run out of reasons to keep living.

The rock he was sitting on was the perfect size for two. He could imagine Kalil sitting there with him. The rock had a bit of a scoop in it, just below where Abdul was sitting, and Kalil would have fit there perfectly. Abdul would have put his arm around Kalil, and Kalil would have rested his head against Abdul's chest, and they would have watched the sea together before starting their new lives in a new land.

Abdul closed his eyes. He could almost feel his friend against him.

It was time for him to move on. Beth would make sure Jonah was all right. Cheslav and Rosalia were both tough. They would find their own way. No one needed him anymore.

So, he was free to leave. He had his medallion back. There was no need even to say goodbye. He would walk into the village, find a road going north and keep walking until he found the bus to Liverpool.

Abdul took one last look at the sea and stood up. He aimed himself in the direction of the village and started walking.

TWENTY

Abdul found the road going north and walked along it with his back to the sea. He walked through two villages until, when the sun started to come up, he came to the town with the National Express coach station. The ticket-seller didn't even look at him as he changed his pound notes into a bus ticket.

He had a two-hour wait. He bought food that he ate without tasting, kept his head down and took no notice of anyone or anything but the clock on the station wall. Then he got in line, eyes on his feet, and took a seat by himself, where he stared without seeing out the window.

He slept for a lot of the journey. People came and sat beside him for longer or shorter stretches, but no one spoke to him and he spoke to no one.

"Liverpool! Norton Street Station! Liverpool! All off at this station!"

A profound sadness sat heavy on Abdul's chest as he left the coach, stepping around the passengers gathering their bags and bundles. He bought a map of Liverpool from a station kiosk. From where he was, he could walk to Penny Lane.

He cried as he walked. He couldn't help it. These were the streets he should have walked with Kalil. This should have been the happiest walk of his life. Instead, it was the loneliest.

Abdul wiped his eyes and consulted his map. It was not far now.

And then, suddenly, he was there. A waist-high sign was bolted to the sidewalk.

Penny Lane.

He put his hand on the sign, oblivious to the passersby, and at that moment he knew he had somehow been expecting Kalil to be there waiting for him. It was as realistic a hope as expecting Lennon and McCartney to be waiting for him on the dock with a spare guitar and an empty chair.

Abdul took the chain with its Yellow Submarine medallion from around his neck. He knelt down by the street sign, brought the medallion to his lips and hung it around the signpost.

And then Abdul was engulfed by an emptiness so profound it robbed his limbs of the ability to support him. There was nowhere to go now. No reason to leave this patch of dirt and concrete. No reason for his heart to keep beating.

His knees came up to his chest and his arms curled around his legs. His back slumped against the sign. His head hung until his face was buried in his knees.

"Hello? Could you move over, please? We're trying to get a picture of the sign."

"Excuse me — you at the sign. Could you move off to the side for us, please?"

"Go up to him, Stanley. Maybe he can't hear you."

"You. I'm talking to you." A hand shook Abdul's shoulder, tentatively at first, then with more force.

"What's this, then?"

"We can handle it. We just want a picture."

"It's one of them bloody foreigners again. There's only one thing they understand." A boot landed in Abdul's side.

"There's no need to…"

"The sign belongs to all of us, doesn't it? Who does he think he is?"

Abdul kept his head down while the debate raged above him. More blows would come soon. They'd get rougher and more painful and he would do nothing to stop them.

"Maybe we should fetch the police."

"Don't need no police to handle this." Another kick, followed by a shove that landed Abdul's face against the pavement.

Kick me in the head, he silently begged.

"All he had to do was move. Really, he didn't need to bring this on."

A boot to his backside tried to shove Abdul along. Abdul could feel the gravel sting his face as it scraped his skin. Someone spat on him.

"Where do they keep coming from? Who keeps letting them into the country?"

Then he heard, "He's with us."

He opened his eyes. Cheslav and Rosalia were there.

"More freaking foreigners," the tough guy said, but he said it into the ground because Rosalia had laid him flat.

"Anyone else want to speak?" she asked, and the crowd of all sorts – hippies, thugs, middle-aged tourists with cameras and Beatles Forever buttons – took a giant step back.

Cheslav took one arm and Rosalia took the other. They raised Abdul to his feet and wiped the dust from his clothes.

"What are you doing here?" Abdul asked.

"You think you are the only one who likes the Beatles?" said Cheslav.

And Rosalia said, "You really are an idiot."

She slipped her arm around his waist. Cheslav did the same, and the three of them, linked together, walked away from the crowd.